Come Sit with Me...

...and listen to stories I want you to hear...

by

George Spain

Ideas into Books®
W E S T V I E W
P.O. Box 605
Kingston Springs, TN 37082
www.publishedbywestview.com

This book is a work of fiction. Names, characters, places and incidents either are products of the author's imagination or are used fictitiously.

ISBN 978-1-62880-037-1

First edition, May 2014

Printed in the United States of America on acid free paper.

Also by George Spain

Lost Cove
Our People: Stories of the South
Delightful Suthun Madness XIII

For My Jackie

Jackie

I want you to be here in the morning,
Warm and well and asleep,
In the bed beside me.

I want you to be here,
Just around the corner in the hall,
In your orange robe and gray slippers.

I want you to be here, so near
I can hear your beautiful voice say,
"Bubbas, is my coffee ready?"

I want you to be here on the couch,
With Sally's head resting on your lap,
And see your hand reach out and pat her.

I want you to be here with me now,
Wiping the tears from my eyes,
So I can see you clearly.

I want you to be here beside me now,
Where I can feel you and hear you,
Saying, over and over, again and again,
"Bubbas, my dear Bubbas, you're so precious."

Table of Contents

...some were really real...

...others were downright ridiculous...

...several were serious...

...and there is one who never leaves me.

Acknowledgments

Thanks to Gayle and Jerry Henderson, Louise Colln, Sally Lee, Carolyn Wilson and to the Williamson County Writers Critique Group for their guidance and support.

Come sit with me

and let me share some tales...

Kids of Summer

Pony

Ride to Glory

Would You Give an Eye to See a...?

The Sword

Road Runner

Kids of Summer

Summer was our heaven:
We were inseparable
as we roamed the fields and woods
of our neighborhood
and downtown Nashville,
our imaginations leading us into
adventures, sometimes in the wrong direction;
teaching us things of life and friendship
which would guide our lives.

Cast of Characters

Billy Bob........ (12) The oldest of our group, our heavily freckled leader ruled over us with his fast fists.

TC.................. (11) When it came to creating disgusting deformities he was the master with his eye lids turned inside out.

Bush............... (11) My best buddy whose devout Catholic family–who drank all kinds of alcohol openly–saved me from many prejudices.

Double M ...... (11) Living all the way over on the next street, he was not quite a full member but he had the best climbing trees and a barn.

GE.................. (10) I was the youngest, the chubbiest and the quickest to come up with ideas for devilment.

Pony

The glob of spit shot out–out–out–and still out until, finally, it curved downward and hit with a SPLAT two feet beyond a battlefield strewn with spittle. Like a warrior king, Billy Bob leaned triumphantly back on his elbows. His was the regal smile of one who has again assured his superiority by right of arms.

It was summertime. The five of us and an assortment of dogs were taking up most of the sidewalk in front of Hutcherson's Pharmacy and Landon's Hardware Store. Our stage. Here, like strolling contortionists, we regularly performed our bad pranks. There was always a passing audience of grownups to be impressed with our ability to spit, or to witness the extraordinary dexterity required when you tightly pressed a thumb against one nostril and loudly blew your nose.

When we ran out of spit and mucus, we would saunter into Landon's. Landon's! Military arsenal and weapons supplier to the summer soldier: BB guns, pocketknives, cap pistols, bows and arrows, sling shots, pea shooters and all the materials you needed to make that *piece de resistance* of summer warfare–rubber guns. Rubber guns fired loops cut from automobile inner tubes. The loops were knotted and stretched tight from the end of the wooden barrel to the clothespin trigger held to the back handle with a band of rubber. Few things in life are more satisfying than hearing the solid whack of knotted rubber hitting the bare back of an enemy playmate. A scream of pain makes it sublime. For the rest of the day, the success of your crafty ambush was there for all to see—a fiery, red whelp. Had we set our ambitions toward cold-blooded mayhem we would have ranked right up there with the Daltons or the Hole-in-the-Wall Gang. As it was, our dogs and cats and younger brothers and sisters constantly watched us out of the corners of their eyes, our creating in their minds ugly sounds and pictures—the rat-a-tat-tat of machine guns riddling criminals full of holes—like Swiss cheese.

Since the dogs and shoppers were bedazzled by our spitting, they deserved an encore. "Let's do our deformities," said TC and immediately began turning his eyelids inside out. Once turned, they could stay that way for hours. Then a silly, pompous grin would spread all across his face. He knew he had the rest of us hands-down when it came to looking deformed. The rest of us weren't even in the same league. Bush could only bend his fingers back to his wrist and my best was your basic lower-leg-out-of-joint walk. But TC was really horrible. You could see it in the startled faces of old ladies who walked hurriedly around us to get in the stores. When you looked at TC dead on, and saw those blood-red strips of raw flesh above the whites of his eyes, it was just about the most sickening thing you can imagine. Today, he wasn't grinning. He had an intense, fixed stare that made him seem totally unaware of the rest of us. When I saw both of his eyelids suddenly flip down, I realized he was experiencing something powerful. I followed his gaze. And then, I saw her....

Standing like a golden statue in the summer sun was a pony standing alone on the school playground across the street. She was stunning—a glowing palomino pony with a flaxen mane and tail—she was the most beautiful thing I had ever seen. A real, live pony—a symbol—nay, the very embodiment of our play: Robin Hood, Mountain Men, Lee, Stonewall Jackson, Tom Mix, cowboys and Indians, warfare of every sort—and through it all we rode straight and strong, striking down our enemies, right and left and—on to victory! High upon that pony's back we would be able to look down on all the rest of humanity—they would be beneath us.

Glitters of light surrounded the pony. Double M, who liked to read stories about the old-timey days, said the glitter looked just like the halo he had seen in a picture of King Arthur's charger. "Gnats, just a bunch of gnats," Billy Bob pronounced. Billy Bob ruled over our gang with the divine right of quick muscles and preferred to dictate the day's visions. "She looks more like something Forrest would have ridden when he whupped up on them damn Yankees." We played Civil War a lot and, of course, he always commanded the winning side—the Rebs. He was either Lee, Jackson or Forrest, and sometimes all three in one battle. He said any dummy could see he had to be the commanding general, since he was the only one who had a Confederate general's hat. It was a cheap, felt thing with a Rhode Island Red chicken feather stuck in the band. He liked to call the feather a plume. While I'll have to admit that the hat had style, the truth is that not one of those generals went around with a plume sticking out of his hat. And if he had, it wouldn't have been an old beat-up Rhode Island Red chicken feather.

The pony had not moved. She was totally alone. She was lost! She was ours for the catching, and ours for the riding. And as we were learning the ways of the world, our minds were already calculating that she represented cold hard cash on the hoof. This gentle beauty had to be some sweet child's dearest possession. We were assured that, loving his child as he did, some rich daddy would offer a reward, would give us money for our good deed. Since she had no halter, Billy Bob told us to go into Landon's and buy some rope. He would keep his eye on the pony. In a flash, we were in and out with the rope. And still the pony was there, as real and as beautiful as ever.

Frantically, we set to work on a lasso. The rope was twenty feet of cotton nightmare. Knot tying is an art, and the only one we had down pat was the standard, impossible-to-untie-except-with-a-sharp-knife-blade shoelace knot. All ten hands started twisting, looping and knotting at the same time. It appeared as if we were trying to come up with the getting-burned-by-rude-rope yanks that gave way to bad name-calling, then to shoving. We were right on the verge of a free-for-all when we stumbled onto it. It looked like something that was half lasso and half hangman's noose. I know this: If I'd been either a horse or a horse thief, I wouldn't have wanted that thing around my neck. But it was going to have to do, or we were going to end up killing each other.

Then, Billy Bob spoke; his words were chilling. "Double M, since you know so much about horses and chargers and stuff, how about you putting that rope around her neck–we'll back you up."

Well now, when it finally gets down to the actual fitting of your imaginings with the realities, they don't always square at the edges. Movies about cowboys and playing cowboys are one thing, but walking right up to a wild stallion and trying to put a rope around his neck, that's another. A sickly look was concentrating itself on Double M's face. I could see his fingers trying to squeeze up and hide in his hands. He began to sag all over as pure fear turned all his bones and muscles to mush. Billy Bob said, "Double M, you ain't goin' chicken on us now, are you?" There it was. Chicken! Better to have bubonic plague, leprosy or only one leg than to be called a "chicken". It was a condemnation worse than death, for it marked you for the rest of your natural-born life. Once you were labeled "chicken" your only options were suicide or moving to another town.

Double M took the rope and, like a man going to his own hanging, struck a death-march pace as we crossed the street. As slow as he was moving, the rest of us were slower. He was our friend, and we wanted him to have plenty of room to run if he needed to. It was like we were in a slow motion film, a classic scene: the King of the Wild Horses is finally cornered. The relentless sun beats down; the five dust-covered cowboys close in; the brave roper moves cautiously up to the horse's head. If the stallion goes for anyone, it will be him; the time of truth has come! The film slows, then stops on a drama-filled scene of the Old West. At the end of a sun-bleached ravine, five sweat-stained cowboys stand, lean and hard, before a great, wild stallion; one cowboy holds a lasso right at the point of passing it over and around the stallion's wide-flared nostrils and chiseled head. And then it happened....

The pony flicked her tail, stomped at a horsefly, curled her lips back from her teeth and gave a long-drawn, high-pitched whinny. Double M screamed, dropped the rope, turned and ran smack-dab into Bush. As we ran, everyone was hollering. I could hear a strange whimpering coming from my throat, and Billy Bob kept saying, "Dear God, save me...dear God, save me."

When we were safely back inside Landon's, and in the back of the store, we turned to see if the frenzied beast was coming straight on through the glass window to kill us all. Double M was so scared he was stuttering, "D-D-Did you see th-those teeth? They c-could have r-r-ripped my arm off my b-b-body!"

Sucking hard for air, Bush gasped, "Those hoofs could have kicked our brains out."

Since the plate glass was holding firm. Billy Bob said, "TC, go up there and see what that thing is doing."

TC said firmly, "Un-uh, I ain't going by myself. You gotta come with me!"

There was a pause, and then Billy Bob said, "OK, everybody, let's go!"

With muscles tensed tight in anticipation of an instant need to leap to safety, we eased up to the window and looked out. The pony had not moved. She stood there, splendid in the sun. For a moment, no one spoke. Then Double M, his voice back to normal, whispered, "Hell, she's just a pony. I'm goin' to get her." With shoulders squared, he went right out the door without looking back. By the time the rest of us were across the street, he had the rope around her neck and she was nuzzling his hand.

For the remainder of the day, we led one another around the schoolyard with one and sometimes two of us sitting on her broad back. Now and then, we would stop to let her rest and graze. As she munched the green grass we lay around her, admiring her gentleness and all of her loveliness. Her golden coat was soft as silk and when for a moment, she raised her head to gaze far away, the peacefulness in her eyes gave us joy. It was a day filled with sun– it was heaven!

A new problem arose as the sun began to set. Now that we had her, where were we going to put her? TC said, "How 'bout Brother Black's?" Brother Black was a Church of Christ preacher who taught at Lipscomb High School where Billy Bob, TC and I were elementary students. He had a field nearby where he kept horses. It was a double-barreled idea. Being that Brother Black, God, Billy Bob, TC and I were so closely tied together it would give Brother Black a chance to do a good deed for everyone. And, as Bush and Double M were Catholics, it would be further proof that the rest of us were on the winning side. Not that we really needed it since their having to eat fish every Friday for eternity was plenty of evidence that God didn't look kindly upon them.

When we got to Brother Black's I volunteered to handle the negotiations. Since the Lord is on the side of the righteous, I wanted the lead position in showing Bush and Double M the error of their ways. The congregation waited behind me in the yard as I offered Brother Black the opportunity to strike a blow for the Lord. And then, with a big smile on his face, that Man of God looked down upon us, and in his best preacher-voice, said, "A dollar a day, boys, a dollar a day. That's what I charge everybody, and to be fair that's what I'll have to charge you, a dollar a day."

What did he say? Did he say a dollar? A dollar a day? He's supposed to say, "God love you, you fine young fellows, bring that beautiful creature of the Lord's right on in here. Bless you for giving me this chance to do good. I won't charge you a cent. For it is written, 'It is more blessed to give than to receive.' Praise the Lord!" What in hell did he just say? A dollar a day? Hell, there ain't a dollar a week among us. Hellfireanddamnation! What he just said was, "No!"

Looking down at my feet, muttering as I stumbled away, "Thanks...we'll see...maybe, thanks a lot." *Hellfireanddamnation, hellfireanddamnation.* As I passed Bush and Double M, I hissed, "If either one of you laugh, or say anything, I'll bust you in the nose."

Pony in tow, we returned to the school yard to think.

As we sat there in the evening shadows, I was sure I heard a snicker and saw some quick smirks pass between Bush and Double M. *Damn the fairness of greedy preachers–now, what are we going to do.*

Finally, Billy Bob spoke up, "Well, we gotta do something and do it quick. The only other place is Mr. Naked's."

We called him "Mr. Naked" because he was an artist who specialized in painting naked women. And if that wasn't bad enough, he had two gosh-awful, gigantic dogs that could kill and eat a grizzly. He lived in an old, run-down house surrounded by vines and hedges. Just thinking about it started my left eye to twitching. My future prospects suddenly took on a bleakness. If I saw one of those naked women, I'd probably go blind; if those beasts saw me, I was going to disappear forever down their throats. But we had to risk it. Mr. Naked was our last chance.

I'd just about had all the excitement I could stand for one day. This time, I wasn't volunteering for anything. The fact was, nobody was. When we pushed our way through those dog-fanged hedges, it was going to be all for one and one for all. *Come on pony.*

We stood before the great walled hedge that surrounded Mr. Naked's house. It was a Dracula scene: the wild, forsaken forest of Transylvania filled with vampires, werewolves and packs of man-devouring dogs. The night was as dark as a wolf's mouth. Bush whispered through his clenched teeth, "You remember those women vampires who slept in those boxes at Dracula's castle...you don't suppose Mr. Naked and those women...."

"Shut up, Bush!" tongue-chopped Billy Bob.

I could tell my hearing was sharpening as we crept through the hedges. Listening for the flap–flap–flap of descending wings. *Can vampires hear your heart booming? Damnit, who keeps stepping on the limbs?* They cracked like dry bones. It was the pony. *I may have to kill her. Better her than me.*

Between the rustle and crackle of our footsteps came a strange, almost imperceptible voice, "Dear Mary Mother of God, forgive me, for I have sinned..."

Then another voice, this one near hysteria, "O' Jesus, I think I smell blood!"

"Damnit, Bush, shut up!" Billy Bob's voice ascending from alto to soprano, struggled against a scream.

We were out, and in the yard. In front of us reared a large ivy-covered, stone house–the castle of Count

Dracula. No one moved, our eyes froze on the iron-hinged front door.

The pony whinnied loudly and pawed the ground.

There before us was the maw of the beast. Light flickered through the door's small windows onto a dragon-headed knocker. The dragon's eyes moved with the light.

I heard my voice praying aloud, in unison with Bush and Double M, "Dear Mary Mother of God, forgive me for I have sinned...Dear Mary Mother of God...."

All I could think of was my throat. When that door opened, how was I going to keep whatever that thing was inside away from my throat? I searched my pockets for a weapon. Nothing. For want of a cross, or some garlic, or a mirror, or a good sharp stake, I was about to be sucked dry.

Listen! "Click"...a lock turned. *O' my Lord, O' my Lord.* The door handle twisted. With the rusty, strident creaking of a coffin lid, the door slowly—ever so slightly—opened.

Standing in the doorway, outlined by the flickering light, was a tall, silent man; his face shadowed.

O' Lord, O' Lord. Children shouldn't have to die this way. Way down, deep inside of me, I felt the last scream of my life beginning to form. *O'Lord, here he...he...he comes.*

"Hello, boys. Can I help you?"

Count Dracula slyly requesting to fang our throats.

We stood there silent, like five stone statues.

"What's wrong? Has a cat got your tongues?"

Dracula the jokester.

He stepped toward us. But—it was just a normal step forward. Not a soaring leap that went straight for my throat. And his voice–it was normal. Not one of those hisses that turn into the last roaring howl you ever hear. It was just a plain ol' everyday voice.

With wide-stretched eyes, we examined him. No wings. No cape. No death-white skin. No burning eyes. NO FANGS! Before our eyes, Count Dracula dissolved... disappeared.

And became...Mr. Naked.

"Whatcha got thah, a pony?" he asked.

"Yes, sir, Mr. Nak...yes, sir, she sure is!" said Bush.

You could see Mr Naked's eyes smiling as he admired her. "She's a beauty. Well, boys, I'm guessin' y'all might be needin' sum help...Y'all are all noddin', 'Yes.' So I'm goin' to guess y'all might need a place for that pony to stay. Right?"

The stars were out as we started home. Once, we stopped to hear the pony whinnying to us through the darkness. Mr. Naked had put her in his field. Then he had taken us into his barn where he fixed an old bridle and saddle for us to use when we rode her. She could stay there until we found her owner. And got our reward. When we asked what he would charge, he just laughed and said, "Boys, I probably ought to be payin' y'all for lettin me keep such a splendid creature." He didn't want a thing. Not a thing. It was free!

As we walked home through that summer night, my mind kept going over and over everything that had happened to us that day. Somehow I knew something important had occurred, something that I could not yet put into words. But later on, way later on, it came to me– *things ain't always the way they appear to be.*

Ride to Glory

Billy Bob was literally eaten up with freckles. In certain kinds of light, his skin looked like he had some gosh-awful tropical disease. A thousand more, give or take a couple hundred, and they would all have run together, turning him into one five-foot tall, skinny freckle. Then we'd have likely ended up calling him "Nig," because he'd have been permanently browned all over. Of course, calling him "Nig" would have made him fiercer than he was prone to be. For my sake, since Billy Bob was older and tougher than me, it probably saved my life by his not being a total freckle.

As I've already said, TC, Bush and Double M made up the rest of our gang. Our acceptance of Double M who lived on the next street was helped considerably by his yard having an old barn that made a first-class clubhouse and a fort when we had BB battles with the Cullum gang who all lived on the other side of Lealand Lane.

Being Catholic, Double M and Bush ate a lot of fish. I've always felt that Fridays must have been hell on them. Maybe I shouldn't admit it, but I got a perverse pleasure when I ate cheeseburgers in front of them on Fridays, which I tried to do with regularity. Admit it, we all like having some solid, here-and-now proof that we bet on the right horse when it comes to religion. Any kid will tell you that eating fish every Friday for the rest of your life is not even close to being in the race when it comes to cheeseburgers. It's a wonder they hung with it. If it had been me, I'd have joined another church just to eat the cheeseburgers.

Back then, in the summertime, kids turned out ideas faster than those Old Testament types begat children. When you haven't got television or air-conditioning, and your mama is committed to teaching you the American Work Ethic, it tends to influence your creativeness in such as getting out of your house without being seen. Those of us who made it, gathered at the "Cussin' Tree."

The Cussin' Tree was a big old mock orange tree that grew green, bumpy, soft-ball-size mock oranges and dripped white sticky stuff when you used them as hand grenades. The tree was hidden in a place like Robin Hood might have had in Sherwood Forest. It's where we went to smoke and talk ugly. And it's where Billy Bob came up with the idea of turning our Red Rider wagons into soapbox racers and riding them through a wall of fire. Democratic-type government wasn't Billy Bob's ambition when he was hot on some new and overpowering idea. At those times, his prepubescent squeak ruled us like a Henry the Eighth bellow, even when we questioned his judgment on things like walls of fire.

By the time we finished the cigarettes that Bush had confiscated from his daddy and pumped ourselves up with some fresh dirty talk, we had Billy Bob's idea roughed out into a plan. I'm telling you, in those days kids were whizzes when it came to creating. If we'd set our minds on better mousetraps, all of us would be rich today.

Come the next day, we replaced the beds of our Red Riders with racing bodies made from wooden crates.

Tied to the front wheel axels were guide ropes that turned them sharper than power steering. Needless to say, Billy Bob's had extra "horse-power," that is, he had built an extension on the back for one of us to kneel on while he pushed.

His idea had come from a *Movietone* film that showed a stunt man smashing his car through a burning barn, then leaping out with his hands clasped high above his head while the crowd roared. As he acted out the leaping, hand-clasping part, I saw a semi-wild, excited look grow on Billy Bob's face, which caused me to tense up. I'd seen it before as I had a flashback to the previous winter when I fell through the ice into Mrs. Foy's goldfish pond. On that day, he had turned us all into north woods trappers. And now, here he was with the same crazy look, telling us all about the glories of riding through a wall of fire.

Double M's street was perfect for setting walls on fire. It had a steep hill, no traffic and, best of all, you couldn't see the bottom of the hill from anybody's house. It took awhile for us to drag a pile of cardboard boxes all the way from the back of Landon's Hardware Store to Double M's street. Billy Bob supervised the wall building. After a lot of adjusting to meet his specifications, it was impressive looking. It was four feet deep, eight feet high and twelve feet wide. From a distance it looked like it would stop a tank.

By now, Billy Bob's movements were starting to get quick all over, like you do when you've just got to take a leak and your surroundings won't allow it. To tell the truth, I was picking up speed too. My muscles were getting jerky and my vision sharper. Now, I was seeing the beauty of it all. That great wall of roaring red, yellow and white flames rising to heaven, and me and Billy Bob riding through it to safety on the other side, where the cheers of the crowds were waiting for us to leap out with our hands clasped high in the air—as HEROES!

No one was going to push Billy Bob's racer but me. For today we were bound for glory.

We waited at the top of the hill; he, forward in the driver's seat, legs squeezed down inside the wooden body, knuckles white from gripping his guide ropes; and me, kneeling on the back, one foot on the ground, one leg bent like a taut bow-string, waiting to shoot toward our target. We waited, our eyes fixed on Bush, "Lighter of the Flame". He lit his newspaper torch and carefully laid the fire around the base of the wall. His movements, the first wisps of flame and smoke, all seemed unreal—slow—silent—sinister, like some ancient preparation for sacrifice. All sound was suspended as I listened for the command. I waited, and then it came: "GO!"

Muscles, bone, nerves, blood, flesh, all that was me released in one mighty heave with such force that, for an instant, the racer's front wheels lifted off the ground, and then we rocketed down the hill. Traveling at a velocity heretofore unknown by a Red Rider, our racer sped down-down-down, with wheels and wind whirling, as though we must lift from the earth into flight. We were a flash of light, rushing toward Billy Bob's fiery vision, which zoomed upward to strike us. Suddenly, for a final split-second, before my face there was a roaring, burning, smothering wall of flame. My last thought was a flash image of a black, burned-to-a-crisp chicken liver—ME!

And then we hit, and were inside all the fire God ever made.

AIR–AIR–cool, cool AIR, free of fire, clean of smoke, quite sweet-tasting–I was out, on the other side, safe and uncharred! I could hear a great, massed cheering from the wonder-struck crowds, and through it all, someone screaming my name. It was Billy Bob. He was on fire! From the top of the wall a single, small box had fallen, flaming, into his lap. He was trapped in the racer and screaming something awful, "Get it off–*get it off–get it off*–GET IT OFF!" With his attention seriously diverted, the racer zig-zagged down the street, gave into a spin, jumped a ditch and overturned. Dust, wisps of smoke, black flakes, and terrible language rose and spread around the wreckage. I had been thrown clear.

TC, Bush and Double M rushed to the racer and dragged Billy Bob out and began rolling him in the dirt. I crawled toward them and slowly climbed up my legs onto my feet. We helped him stand and began to do our best to separate the dirt and gravel and black bits of charred cardboard from his flesh. He seemed to be totally unappreciative of our efforts, for between groans and whimpers, he'd flail one of us, then another, with the worst cussin' I'd ever heard. But we stuck steady to our task. We all knew there would be hell to pay if Billy Bob went home and his mama looked at him and he didn't look right. For all of our mamas were sworn to some unwritten, but binding, maternal pact of perversity to telephone each other whenever they knew, or even suspicioned that we had been up to no good. For they knew us, they knew that we had a righteous obligation to share with one another the joys of our sins.

All in all, Billy Bob began looking better, especially after we had spit on our hands and cleaned his face. Double M kept brushing hard with some leaves on a big black spot on his t-shirt until he was rudely pushed away. We stood back to observe our handiwork.

Everyone had hope on his face, especially Billy Bob. Like an artist seeking the slightest flaw on a finished portrait, we looked him up and down.

Nobody moved or spoke. The very silence suggested something dreadful. I looked at TC, then Double M and Bush. Their eyes were stretched big-wide, and the skin on their faces had gone white, loose and scary. I got a sudden queasy, sick feeling, like a knife was twisting in the pit of my stomach. I looked again at Billy Bob, and there before me was the awful truth of a fiery ride.

Billy Bob's eyebrows were burned plumb off his face.

Would You Give an Eye to See a…?

It was our very last Friday before the end of summer vacation; our last three days of freedom; our last three days before we returned to the fiery pit; our last three days before our parents forced us back to school.

We were sprawled on the ground beneath the ‘Cussin Tree'. Hidden from the spying eyes of grownups by wild hedges and bushes; it’s where we went to smoke and talk ugly and plot and scheme against the unfair rules of grownups. It’s also where we learned from one another some of the facts of life, wonderfully distorted though they so often were. We’d just finished a close examination of the Women’s Underwear section in the Sears Roebuck catalogue that I had brought and were smoking away on the Camels Billy Bob had confiscated from his father. Everyone’s face was serious.

“Well, we’d better make tha best outta tomorrow,” said Bush.

“Damn right bout that,” said TC.

“Double damn right bout that,” said Double M.

“Well, we better come up with somethin good, cause ya’ll know what comes after tomorrow,” I said.

Except for school days, Sunday mornings were the most horrible part of the week. God could have done a whole lot better when He made it. Every Sunday morning we had to pay for our sins of smoking, lying, stealing, cursing and for–well you know–what boys do at night under the covers. Penance began with scrubbed faces, slicked-down hair, starched shirts, itchy suits and ties so tight they could have strangled a Silverback Gorilla to death.

Church was ninety percent boredom and ten percent pure terror. Most preachers weren't worth a tinker's damn when it came to holding a kid's attention. But it's sort of funny, for the older I've gotten the more appreciation I've had for all those years of being bored to death in church. I think it helped me out in life. During the half hour the preacher droned on and on I would sit there dreaming up all kinds of stuff in my head that might keep me out of school for a few days—things like breathing in a lot of dust and having an attack of asthma or drinking enough soapy water to make me vomit or getting a dog to bite me. Church was a hothouse that nurtured the imagination of my youth.

Then there were those ten-percent times of terror. These were usually during revivals, which were held at least once a year and more often if the elders thought the congregation's attention wasn't focused enough on the Final Judgment or that the numbers were slipping on baptisms and restorations. They'd bring in some fire-and-brimstone big name who could scare the daylights out of adults and terrorize the children. He'd get so worked up you could taste sulfur in the air and see the Devil's face reflected in his eyes. Sometimes I couldn't look I'd get so scared. A couple of times I wet my bed at night.

My preference was stories from the Old Testament; those filled with throwing people to lions, walls of water drowning millions of Egyptians, dogs eating women, and Samson killing a ton of Philistines with the jawbone of an ass. These stories kept me wide-awake with my eyes and ears glued on the preacher. But I paid for it at night. The sounds and pictures of all that screaming and blood and death would creep into my bedroom and scare me so bad I'd cover my head with the sheet and pray out loud until I fell asleep. I think these gory sermons influenced my later love of horror stories and movies and some of my own gory writings. So church wasn't entirely wasted on me.

Thank the good Lord my family was Church of Christ. If they'd been Catholic I would have been dead before I was eight years old. I had asthma. Breathing all that smoke pouring out of those little buckets the priests swung around and around over everybody's heads sure as anything would have smothered me to death right there in my pew. And as to being an alter boy–un-huh–dressing up like a girl in a long white gown and carrying big, tall things and chanting in Latin would have been worse than what I was up against in our church.

Speaking of Latin, I need to say something about its effect on my life. I tried it out for two years in high school and for two years it gave me a splitting headache. I suffered just like the saying goes, "Latin is a dead language, as dead as can be. First, it killed the Romans, now it's killing me." It would have been easier on my brain to have pounded my head against a rock than against Caesar's Gallic Wars. I made two years of straight Ds. When I reminded Ms. Whitten, my Latin teacher, of this at our fiftieth high school reunion she tried to reassure me with the comforting words, "But, George, they were all good Ds."

So there we were under the Cussin' Tree trying to come up with a good plan for living it up on Saturday. One dumb idea after another had been shot down when

TC who was leaning back on his elbows sat up, took a deep draw off his cigarette and said, "I'll tell you what we oughta do, there's a double feature at tha Princess an they're showing Strangler Of The Swamp and Isle Of The Dead with Boris Karloff...Man, ya can't beat Karloff for our last day on earth together." TC was prone to speak in extremes and loved horror movies more than he loved his little sister. He saw he had our attention. He took another deep draw, paused dramatically, looked slowly around at each of us, then said, "Hell, ya'll know there's only one place for us to go...we gotta spend tha whole day downtown."

While he wasn't known for having good ideas, the moment TC said it, we all knew he had knocked the ball out of the park. Downtown it was!

Downtown Nashville was our playground and one of our schools of life. We roamed it. We explored it. We tasted and smelled it. Nooks and crannies, every alley, every stairwell, every rooftop held something new; at times, it was something disturbingly glorious, then at others we discovered something so horrible it returned in the dark of the night, hovering above our beds. The city was filled with blind musicians, beggars, all shades of colored people, parades of women with mink around their shoulders, men in pin-striped suits and two-toned shoes and a man without legs rolling down the sidewalk on a small wooden shelf attached to roller skates.

If we didn't ride the bus to town, my father would drive us in one of his shiny Cadillacs to his car lot on Broad, two blocks from the heart of downtown. None of the other fathers had cars approaching anywhere near my dad's Cadillacs.

From his lot we headed into the heart of the city like a small band of Cherokee searching and hunting for whatever prey was unfortunate enough to cross our path.

First and foremost was Harvey's, Nashville's largest and newest department store. It had everything: real live monkeys in a cage beside a soda fountain, a carousel, clowns and, most special of all, the city's first escalators. Six floors high, we could spend a good couple of hours there running up the escalators going down and down those going up, playing hide-and-seek, cramming all five of ourselves into elevators full of women shoppers and examining naked female mannequins.

From Harvey's, we advanced, side-by-side, up the sidewalk to the State Museum beneath the War Memorial building. The Museum contained two of Tennessee's greatest possessions: big glass jars of formaldehyde with things in them–horrible things–that looked like babies. The other was an Egyptian mummy that was just a little older than our grandparents.

We could hardly take our eyes off the things floating in the jars.

Bush whispered, "Oh my gosh, are those real babies?"

"You dummy!" said TC, "Can't you see they ain't babies, they're aliens. I saw some that looked just like em in *Monsters From Mars.* My dad says they're everywhere out in New Mexico. Flying saucers land out there all tha time an my dad says that tha government keeps it a big secret. These must have been some that got away an got run over on the highway an somebody from Tennessee found em and picked em up an contributed em to the Museum. Hell, they might even have come from somewhere up in tha Smokies. I bet they land up there too."

"Oh my gosh! I ain't ever goin to tha Smokies again."

"Yep, that's exactly what they are. They're aliens!"

Bush was beginning to look a little queasy, like he might throw up. I guess he would have if Billy Bob hadn't brought us back down to earth with a sharp finality, "Hells-fire-an-damnation ya'll, let's go look at tha mummy."

The mummy mesmerized Billy Bob. I believe he would have skipped going to a movie or eating Krystals just to stand there and stare at it, especially where its sex parts were or, at least, where they should have been; as far as I could tell whatever had been there a million years before had dried up and fallen off. Every time he looked at it, his eyes would bulge and start shining and his face would turn red and now and then his body would quiver and every time he'd say the same thing, "Ya'll, look-a-there. Look-a-there. Look at his weenie. Look at his weenie!" And he'd be pointing with his finger and it would be jerking back and forth like it was going straight through the glass.

His voice would rise higher and higher and we'd tell him to hush up or a guard would come in. And one time one did. He stared at us for a minute then asked, "What's goin on here?" We were so scared nobody answered. I could see he was studying Billy Bob the hardest. I think he figured it all out quickly because he stuck his thumbs in his gun belt and nodded toward Billy Bob, "OK, you fellows get on outta here right now an be sure an take him with you. We don't want his type hangin around here." Double M and Bush got behind Billy Bob and shoved him ahead of us until we got outside. Once the sun and air hit him he began to come back.

Next stop was the State Capitol. While not quite as exciting as the Museum, it had its points. There was a real dead man in its walls. First thing, we'd go to the exact spot where his bones were or whatever was in there, and put our ears up against the stone to listen for any sound at all. Then we'd put our hands on the stone to see if it was cooler than the others, for that was a sure sign a ghost or spirit was there.

Though horror movies sometimes made TC wet his bed, he loved Poe as much as he loved Count Dracula and Frankenstein movies. Before he said it, I knew exactly what was going to come out of his mouth because I'd read everything Poe had written, too.

"I betcha he was buried alive in there!"

Double M leaned forward and put his ear against the stone. All of us held our breaths and watched. For a minute nothing happened. Then, his lips stretched away from his teeth, his eyes bulged, his face contorted and a guttural rasping came from deep in his throat. Bush was standing right beside me; I heard a faint voice, almost as though it had no breath, "Oh my gosh...Oh my gosh...that thing's in there an it's alive...."

Just as Bush said, "That thing's in there an it's alive," Double M shoved back away from the wall, leaped into the air with his face like a madman's, his hands like claws and screeched, "YAAEEEeeeeee!"

It scared me so bad I squnched my eyes and covered my face with both hands.

Then he began laughing loudly and I heard a 'thud.'

"Damn, that hurt!" cried Double M.

"Well, that's for you bein a damn fool," said Billy Bob.

I took my hands away and opened my eyes.

Double M was rubbing his right shoulder where Billy Bob had hit him. TC was rising from a crouch where he had folded his arms over his head for protection. Bush was nowhere to be seen.

Ten minutes later we found him hiding in the men's restroom. For a long while he refused to come out of the stall. It took all of us to convince him that it was just another of Double M's sick jokes. Finally, the stall door opened slowly and Bush peeked out. He looked both ways, and seeing there was no moldy dead man in the room he stepped out. Glaring at Double M, he hissed, "You're sick!" and walked out of the restroom.

Before we left the Capitol we went inside and took a quick look at the chipped place on the marble handrail beside the wide steps that led up to the Senate and House Chambers; the crack was made by one politician shooting at another and missing. Every time we stuck our fingers in the crack we were disappointed no one had been killed.

From the Capitol we descended upon the Bennie Dillon building; it was twelve stories high. There were two things that drew us to that building every time we were downtown: the stairwell and the rooftop.

From the top floor of the stairwell was a ten-inch opening between the handrails all the way down to the ground floor. From the top floor you could see hands on the railing as people came up the steps. The goal was to spit and hit the hand. Nine out of ten times we missed but on the tenth, when you struck your target and heard the horrified scream of a woman or the loud cursing of a man, it was better than making an A in Latin. Because of my asthma and congestion I tended to have several gallons more mucus than the others, thereby making me, hands down, the champion spitter–it was usually my spit that hit.

If you hit a man as old as Methuselah or one with a bad leg all you'd get was a lot of ugly language; but if you hit a man who could still run up steps, the next thing you'd hear was pounding footfalls as he came tearing upward shouting, "When I catch you I'm going to rip your mouth out, then I'm going to kill you."

Then, like Bush, at the Capitol, we would flee to the nearest restroom and hide in the stalls, even if we all had to cram into one. There we waited, not breathing, not talking, praying silently; after a half day or so, if it was quiet, we'd send the one who'd hit the hand out to see if the assassin was gone. If so, we'd go back and spit awhile more until our spit ran out. Then we would go to the rooftop.

We knew almost every unoccupied part of the Bennie Dillon Building. The rooftop was the most special spot of all. From there you could see the river and barges, the distant tree covered hills; leaning over the low brick wall at the edge you could see the shoppers, they scurried back and forth like ants, in and out of holes, twisting their antennas, telling one another where they had just bought this or that, or had just eaten that or this, and then they scurried on to other holes and other ants.

As there was a strong desire within me to live, I was terrified about standing anywhere near the edge of anything over twelve feet high. Twelve stories into the sky was the next thing to being on Everest without any ropes around you. The nearer I got to the edge of the rooftop the more my imagination took hold. A malignant force drew me forward. To avoid being called 'chicken' I would ease up to it, barely lifting my feet, and look over the side then quickly step back. In that one glance down through the clouds to the earth far below I could see myself toppling over that little bitty, frail wall and screaming for thirty minutes before I hit the sidewalk. And I could hear my dear mother weeping and see my father shaking his head at the stupidity of his idiot son.

Billy Bob was in the lead as we climbed the last steps to the door that opened onto the roof. As he put his hand on the knob he turned and looked at me, "Well, Spain, are you going to jump this time?" He, like the rest of us, had a twisted sense of humor. The others laughed, I looked at my feet, as Billy Bob's hand turned the knob and the door began to open.

At this point, I need to pause and explain about a game we played at the Cussin' Tree. We'd be lying on the ground around it, leaning back on our elbows, smoking and telling dirty jokes when all of a sudden one of us would say, "Hey, ya'll, would you give an eye to see a...?" and then he'd say something so gross or obscene it can't be repeated here; if it was really awful we'd hold our noses and make gagging sounds. But if it was something that was sexually graphic and we could see it, we'd sit up and lean toward the speaker with our eyes stretched wide and excited and begin to talk all at once, "My gosh, say that all over again...damnation that's, that's...oh my, oh my...you know anymore like that?" When you got that reaction you were, hands down, the gross subject champion for the day! And for certain, someone would say, "Well, I'd give an eye to see that."

Billy Bob pushed the door all the way open and, one by one, we stepped out into the bright sunlight. For a moment we couldn't see a thing and then, suddenly, we could see. *Oh my goodness! Oh my goodness!* was all my mind could say. My entire body filled with electricity. If souls can quiver I think mine quivered so hard it left my body.

For a boy—and a thousand times more for a man—there's nothing God placed on this earth that comes anywhere near equaling the body of a woman who is almost naked. It is absolutely why the words 'frenzied anticipation' were created. All we hoped for. All we prayed for. Our very reason for existing.

There before us, stretched out on a towel, was a woman sunbathing in her underwear.

I clamped my hands over my eyes so fast and hard I almost broke my nose. I stopped breathing. Time passed. There was a great silence. More time passed. And then I heard my voice speak to me in my head, '*Would you give an eye to see an almost naked woman?*' There was not the slightest hint of a pause as my voice answered, '*Yes! Oh, yes, I would!*' And as it spoke I said a quick prayer, opened my left eye and peeped between my fingers.

Long years have passed since that glorious day of sunshine and still I quiver in frenzied anticipation when I see with my two good eyes an almost naked woman. Thank you, God, for Your never-ending mercies!

The Sword In The Attic

It was 1946. The war was over. It was summer in the land of the free. School was out, the sun was shining and not one of us—not even I—had to go to summer school. As a reward, the Lord had sent us a gift; a new street was being built a half mile from our homes. Bulldozers were already digging up the earth and somewhere in all that dirt, hidden treasures were waiting for us.

The day was hotter'n hell; you could swim in the humid air. None of our houses had air-conditioning; as soon as we could escape from our mothers we were gone, sometimes for a whole day.

We gathered with our bikes in Billy Bob's backyard. Except for our shorts, we were naked. If not for being reported to our parents by little old do-gooder ladies, we would have gone naked as soon as we were out of sight of our houses.

Billy Bob's freckles were growing by the hundreds every day the sun shined and that was everyday. Though I never breathed it aloud, I thought he looked like a colored man with some kind of gosh-awful jungle disease. Double M and Bush were Catholic which I figured was the reason their skins burned so easy. TC and I were the only ones with nice tans, me because I had some Indian blood; I don't know where TC's came from.

The new street was next to a big field where Brother Black kept horses. The summer before, Brother Black, a preacher and teacher at the Church of Christ school which TC, Billy Bob and I attended, had tried to beat us out of a dollar a day to keep a lost pony we'd found. All of our allowances together didn't make a dollar a day. As we had walked away with the pony TC whispered, "Scrooge." I whispered back, "He's *a tight-fisted old craphead.*" Double M and Bush had smirks on their faces, seeing it was a blow for the side of the Catholics.

When we got to where the bulldozers had been digging, we spread out and began to circle like five sharp-eyed buzzards searching the up-turned earth for a dead rabbit or dog or, better yet, a cat. Our anticipation was probably better than anything we were likely going to find on the ground half-covered with dirt. Hopeful anticipation is one of the things that helps you get up in the morning; if you don't have it, then you might as well roll over and go back to sleep. Or die.

One of the best things about living in the South is all the dead people in the ground; they are everywhere: dead Indians, dead soldiers and just plain old dead people. Now and then, some lucky kid or archeologist would hit the jackpot; better than finding bones of dead people was finding bones of a prehistoric beast, especially something really big like a saber tooth tiger, or a giant bear or a mastodon. Finding one of these would sure as anything get your picture in the paper and turn your playmates green with envy.

My dream was to find a stone box grave with a complete Indian skeleton and a lot of gold jewelry; or a rusty bayonet with dried blood on it or a rifle barrel, even a Minie ball; anything that had killed a Yankee. It would have been better than making straight As all year long and having a string of gold stars by your name. Finding a stone box grave that hadn't been messed up by a dozer or a stupid grownup was the kind of thing that created such excitement that it almost made you wet your shorts or start a shoving match to see who got first dibs on what was inside.

It was Saturday. No one was working. We had all the dug-up earth to ourselves. The only others were a bunch of sparrows scratching and pecking. We spread out, peering and sniffing at the ground. Occasionally, someone would shout and we'd run to them; our anticipations leaping us across the stones and clods to reach the shouter—and to nothing but an old tennis shoe or an Orange Crush bottle. I thought Billy Bob was going to hit Double M with a rock when Double M hollered because a bee had stung him. Billy Bob had little sympathy for us when we were in pain. "You sissy, spit on it and quit whining," was all the compassion and medical treatment Double M was going to get.

We'd been there about an hour, getting dirtier and dirtier, and tireder and thirstier by the minute, when all of a sudden, Bush gave a shout and enough "Damns" it made us know we'd better come running, "DAMN...DOUBLE DAMN! Ya'll look what I found! DAMNATION! DAMNATION!"

We stood around him in a circle and looked down. Six inches beyond our toes we could see the top of two broad stones. In various tones, we all echoed, "DAMNATION!" as we looked down at the top of what we were certain was a stone box grave. We had seen pictures of them in books and read in newspapers about people finding them but none of us had ever seen one in real life, much less found one.

The two slabs were clearly outlined beneath a thin covering of dirt. We waited for Billy Bob's orders. He was our leader because of his fast fists, which all of us had felt at one time or another.

Finally, he spoke, "Well, I'll be damn!"

We all nodded.

"Well, you guys quit standin there, get down an clean it off."

On our hands and knees we worked swiftly as though he had a bullwhip cocked above us ready to flay our naked backs. With a quick stirring of dust up into our eyes and nostrils, it was done.

"OK, OK, get back an let me do tha liftin so nothin goes wrong."

We stood up and took a couple of steps back and watched.

He squatted at the far end of the largest stone, reached out, crooked his fingers in the crack between the two stones, took a deep breath and began to stand, pulling the stone upward. His eyes and cheeks bulged; the places where he wasn't freckled turned red and he made a strange sound, like something was boiling inside his mouth. I thought his head was going to explode and splatter all over us.

Then it happened...the stone slipped from his hands and he fell backwards into the dirt.

We watched as it fell in slow motion–down–down–down. For a second, there was silence. No one breathed. No birds sang. The clouds did not move. The heat waves stopped rising.

The end of the world will sound like the sound that was made as the stone crashed back into the grave. There was a sharp cracking of bones and pottery, and the startled flapping of sparrows' wings as they burst upward and above these were our cries to God for mercy.

The dust blinded us. A little more and we would have smothered to death. No one moved, not even to help Billy Bob to his feet. No one spoke. We were struck dumb. All we could feel was a dreadful fear. We were frozen in a black and white photograph of people long dead.

"Well, who'n hell's goin to help me up?"

Bush and TC pulled Billy Bob to his feet.

The dust was still so thick we couldn't see into the grave.

We waited.

And waited.

Finally, the air cleared. We stepped forward and peered down into the grave. What we saw was so far beyond disbelief no word has yet been created for it. The only thing that could have done more damage to the skeleton and pottery would have been six sticks of dynamite. All that remained was dust and the crumbs of the skeleton and pottery.

There was total silence. I think Billy Bob could see inside our heads. What he saw wasn't pretty. If he had spoken we would have killed him right then and there and stuffed his body into the grave, filled it in with dirt and rocks and smoothed it over on top. Then we would have made a pact to never tell anyone, dusted ourselves off, gotten on our bikes and ridden home for lunch.

All we got were a few teeth and finger bones. I drilled holes in mine and made a necklace, I still wear it sometimes on Halloween.

Ten minutes later we were at Bush's house. We were starving. Mr. and Mrs. Miller, his parents, were gone for the day. Before I go on, I should explain that the world opened up to us when any of our parents were gone from home for a good part of the day. It was like going to Treasure Island. We searched our parentless houses better than the F.B.I. could have. Attics, basements, refrigerators, closets, under beds and pretty much anything closed that wasn't chained and padlocked was ours to find, to look into, to touch, to eat and even drink–and more, much more. We saw things we were not supposed to see, some we did not understand; we discovered relatives we had not known existed, some beautiful, some who looked like gangsters; and we learned of good things and bad things that brought smiles, sniggers and silence.

In the Millers' kitchen we turned into locusts. We drank all the milk, ate a whole loaf of bread, a jar of peanut butter, a jar of grape jelly and finished off all the cookies in the cookie jar. Then we went to the den in the basement. Bush flipped the lights on. What a den it was! With its large stone fireplace and pine paneled walls covered with photographs. The chairs and couch were covered with big cushions. But what made it the most special den I had ever seen was the bar and bar stools in the corner. On the wall, behind the bar, were three shelves filled with bottle after bottle of scotch, gin, vodka, bourbon, brandy, sherry and stuff I'd never heard of. The rows of gleaming glasses, their sparkling reflections of light and the different colors of liquor and the varied shapes of bottles and labels were the next thing to any decorated Christmas tree I had ever seen. We couldn't take our eyes off of them.

Before anyone else made a sound, Bush said, "Ya wanta drink?"

Bush's family, the Millers, were genetically Catholic, which leads into the world of theology, a world where people lose their tempers easily and tend to get a lot of satisfaction out of shortcomings in those who believe differently than they do.

A good example is what I knew about Catholics:

1. They were condemned to eat fish every Friday for eternity.
2. They baptized babies by sprinkling water on their heads instead of totally shoving them underwater.
3. They had to sit in little closets and tell awful things about themselves and then a priest they couldn't even see would give them a lot of boring stuff to do and say.
4. They had to do what they were told by the Pope who couldn't even speak good English, if at all, and wore a long robe instead of a suit and tie, like grown preachers should. Also, he wanted to take over the United States.
5. In school the nuns beat the hell out of boys' knuckles and palms.
6. They liked to drink and dance and gamble and have lots of children.
7. When they died they might have to hang around in a strange place for a long time before they ended up in heaven or hell.

8. They had a secret men's club called the Knights of Columbus where they took an oath to kill all kinds of people, most especially Masons. My father was a Mason.

When I'd say these things–except the part about killing–to Bush and Double M, they'd start getting offended and try to argue with me, but nothing they said held any water since I had heard the truth direct from the mouths of my preachers and teachers.

I never showed Bush or Double M my authentic copy of the oath members of the Knights of Columbus had to take. It had been given to us at school. It was long and went on and on until it finally reached the really good part:

"I do further promise and declare that I will, when opportunity presents, make and wage relentless war, secretly and openly against all heretics, Protestants and Masons...I will secretly use the poison cup, the strangulation cord, the steel of the poniard, or the leaden bullet...that I will provide myself with arms and ammunition that I may be in readiness when the word is passed, or I am commanded to defend the church either as an individual or with the militia of the Pope...

"In testimony hereof, I take this most holy and Blessed Sacrament of the Eucharist and witness the same further with my name written with the point of this dagger dipped in my own blood and seal in the face of this Holy Sacrament."

There it was in black and white. The first time I read it, it scared me so bad I dreamed that night about Mr. Miller strangling my father with a green and gold cord. I never showed the oath to anyone, especially my parents; I kept it hidden in the bottom of the cardboard box that held my comic books. I think I was afraid if my parents saw it, especially my father, it would somehow make it come true and would result in him being poisoned, or strangled or run through with a dagger.

And it was going to be done by Mr. Miller. He was one of them. He was a member of the Knights of Columbus. The year before I was given the copy of the oath, Mr. Miller had taken Bush and me with him to the white, two-story Knights of Columbus building; right up the steps and in the front door and then through another door that opened into a high-ceilinged room the size of a basketball court. He spoke to everybody and they spoke to him. They all seemed to be friends. They all called him "Johnny."

My eyes stretched as wide as they could go. The room they called 'The Hall' was a wonder to behold: slot machines, pinball machines, roulette tables, card tables and crap tables were everywhere. On the walls were paintings of men wearing dark blue robes and feathered hats, several with swords. Above the paintings, flagpoles slanted outward, some with American flags; others were gold and blue with green crosses on them. From the rafters hung blue banners with gold lettering, many with the symbol of an ax head, sword and what looked like an anchor. At the far end, above the fireplace, were two crossed swords with silver blades and golden handles. Through an open door I could see a dimly lit room with a bar and tables where men were drinking and laughing. But what made me really stop and stare were two priests: one shooting dice, the other spinning a roulette wheel.

I remember little else, not even how long we were there. The strangeness of it scared me a little and I moved closer to Mr. Miller, yet there was a part of me, a large part of me, thrilled by it all.

Mr. Miller loved beer–Miller beer. He traveled all across middle Tennessee as a newspaper distributor. In the summer, he often took Bush and me with him. Everyday, at lunchtime, he would take us to the best place in whatever town we were in that served good hamburgers, french fries and ice-cold beer. He always drank draft beer in a mug bigger than a soup bowl. Sitting across from him, I could hardly take my eyes off the white foam above the amber beer and the icy skim on the mug. It looked almost as good as a chocolate milkshake. When he drank, it made a white streak above his upper lip like a mustache, and when he salted it the foam rose like magic. He was a good man who liked to tease me, laugh and tousle my hair. He and Mrs. Miller and all their family were always kind, treating me as one of them. It was from them and from my parents that I eventually learned that kindness can be greater than a lie and sometimes, kindness is even greater than religion. But that day had not yet come when I was ten years old.

"Well, do ya'll wanta drink?"

The words had barely gotten out of Bush's mouth the second time when we all shouted, "YES!"

"OK," he said, "Wait a minute." He ran from the room and up the steps and was back in an instant with an empty coke bottle filled with water and a funnel and towel. "I'll be tha bartender an do tha mixin, since it's my liquor an my bar."

With that, he turned and took down every open bottle. There were seven of them. Next, he got a tall glass and poured maybe four or five thimbles full from each bottle into the glass and then he put the funnel in each mouth and replaced the exact amount taken out with water, put the top back on, wiped the bottle off, shook it a little and placed it back in its exact place on the shelf. He repeated this seven times. Totally concentrated on his concoction, he never looked up, never said a word. It was like watching a movie of a great scientist in his laboratory turning out a cure for Billy Bob's jungle disease. We were in awe. I knew of no Church of Christ boy who had anywhere near this kind of genius. He was so good at it, it made me think he had done it before.

After the last bottle was back on the shelf, he took a spoon from under the bar and briskly stirred everything together. He held the glass close to his eyes. When it was mixed to his satisfaction, he looked up and said, "What'll we call it?"

Billy Bob said, "How bout 'Witches' Brew'?" which didn't have any imagination at all.

"Or 'Vampire Blood'?" said TC who still wet his bed after seeing a Bela Lugosi or Lon Chaney movie.

"Or, how bout 'Seven Farts to tha Wind', said Double M who had a thing about saying fart, and was always trying to work the word in no matter how inappropriate it was.

The night before, I'd been to the movies with my parents. We'd seen a John Wayne war film that had left me feeling patriotic on the inside, "No, you guys, they ain't any good. Since we just beat the hell out of the Germans an Japs let's call it the 'Victory Drink'."

The others squnched their noses up and turned their thumbs down.

Then, with finality, Bush spoke, "Look, you guys, since I made it and I'm the bartender, I'll name it. I once heard my daddy say the name of a drink that beats tha hell outa anything ya'll have come up with...It's a 'Singapore Sling'."

So it was named.

"OK, Bush," said Billy Bob, "Since you named it, how bout you goin upstairs an gettin some cigarettes for us to smoke with it."

Immediately, we all backed Billy Bob with our "Uh-huhs."

It was clear Bush didn't like it, but he got up and went back upstairs. This time he was gone longer. When he came back, he held his hand out and opened it; there were four half cigarettes and one whole one which he immediately put in his mouth, "The halves are yours, take it or leave it!"

We took our halves, then we all lit up and Bush poured the drinks, about four tablespoons each. With that, we sat down on the soft cushions, leaned back and, like soldiers of fortune in a Bogart film, smoked our cigarettes and sipped our martinis.

Ten seconds later, coughs, gags, hacking, red faces and a lot of "Damns" filled the room. And the Bogart film ground to a halt.

When we finished spitting into the bar's sink we got some soap and washed our mouths out, to remove the slightest trace of Singapore Sling. We smelled each other's breath until we were certain our mothers could not pick up the slightest scent of our sin. To get Billy Bob back for destroying our skeleton, Bush and I told him we could still smell a little alcohol on his breath, so he should wash his mouth a second time.

In our church, drinking alcohol was right up there with murder, fornication, mixed swimming and dancing. It could send you straight to hell. Billy Bob, TC and I didn't have one of those places like Bush and Double M where you could hang around for a while—we just went straight on to hell. Of course, all of us would end up in hell on earth if our mothers found out we'd been drinking and smoking.

After we'd cleaned up all the traces of our binge, we still had a couple of hours before the Millers returned home. We went to the second floor and began to systematically look in all the drawers and closets, with particular attention given to the room of Bush's older sister.

We saved the attic for last. It was narrow and long and smelled of mothballs. It was full of stuff: winter clothes, Christmas decorations, boxes of cards, letters and photographs, luggage and more boxes on top of boxes.

Halfway into the attic, a glint of light above me caught my eye. I looked up. Two shelves ran the length of the right side of the room. On the highest shelf I could see the edge of a silver strip of metal. I pointed to it, "Bush, what's that?"

He looked and in a rather off-handed tone said, "O that, that's my father's Knights of Columbus sword."

I almost fainted, *O my God, that's what Mr. Miller is going to use to cut my daddy's head off with.* I could feel my left eyelid twitching; all my breath caught in my throat; I might not breathe or speak again.

Bush turned around and looked at me, "What's wrong with you? Are you sick? You better not vomit in here."

Billy Bob punched me in the back. It hurt like hell but started me to breathing and talking again, "Can I see the sword?"

"Yeah, but you got to swear on your mother's grave not to vomit."

"I swear on her grave." I said.

Bush looked at Billy Bob, "Can you reach it?"

Billy Bob was a full head taller than me. He was the tallest of all of us and lean as a beanpole. He stood on his toes, stretched his long arms and fingers; all of him was just enough to reach the sword's scabbard and lift it down.

Bush took it from him, gripped the handle and pulled the sword from its scabbard and held the blade up to the ceiling light. It glistened like Excalibur.

The second I saw it; I knew it could cut my father's head off. It was long, silvery and sharper than hell. I wanted to hold it. But before I could ask, Bush slid the sword back into the scabbard and gave it to Billy Bob, who put it back on the shelf.

Then, it was time to go home.

As the years passed we went our separate ways. The Millers moved away first; then TC and his family; after Billy Bob and Double M graduated from high school and went off to college, we might run into each other every year or so. We'd talk a few minutes and make promises to get together and bring each other up-to-date. We never did. I made new friends, as I'm sure they did. Slowly, I forgot them. But then, a few years back, when I started writing they suddenly came into my mind. I wrote a story about the five of us called *Pony*, followed by *Ride To Glory* and now, as I write *The Sword In The Attic*, I see us clearly again: half-naked, sitting around our Cussin' Tree, smoking and telling our newest dirty jokes; driving our Soap Box racers through cardboard walls of fire; riding the lost pony that was the color of pure gold; I hear our laughter and "Damnations" as we shoot one another on our bare backs with rubber guns; and, for a little while, we are together again.

How (With A Little Help) My Father Captured The Notorious Car Thief And Escape Artist "Road Runner" Rigsby

For more than twenty years, "Road Runner" Rigsby was the premier car thief and escape artist of Middle Tennessee. Toward the end of Road Runner's career a reporter, interviewing him in the Davidson County Jail, asked how many cars he had stolen. He answered, "Well, that's sorta hard to put an exact number to...let's just say it was quite a few dozen or so over a hundred...ya know, when we're born, tha good Lord gives us all a gift an I guess I was lucky 'cause He gave me two: stealin cars an fast feet." It was the latter gift that led the police and newspapers to nick-name him "Road Runner". Police Chief Jesse Rhett, a close friend of my father, said, "Houdini didn't hold a candle to him. You'd think you had him one minute and the next he'd take off running and our fastest officers couldn't catch him on foot; even the young ones running him in relay couldn't lay a hand on him. Damn, that man could run! I came on him stealing a 1969 Corvette out on Murfreesboro Road near the Asylum an when he saw me he took off running in the grass beside the road...I clocked him for a stretch and I'll be damned if he didn't just about hit twenty-five miles per hour, then he jumped the fence over into a cornfield and was gone. If he hadn't smoked like a chimney he could have hit thirty flat out. I'll tell you one thing, he'd have been hell on the Gold Medals in the Olympics."

His real name was Nathan Bedford Forrest Rigsby. He grew up poor in “The Barrens”, a heavily forested, sparsely settled part of Williamson County that stretched for miles along Backbone Ridge and the Natchez Trace. It was a semi-lawless area known for its production of good whiskey, cock fighting and, on occasion, a killer or two. Independence–not book law–was the rule that guided those who lived there. Road Runner told my father, “Livin in Tha Barrens had its good points an its bad but after tha Revenuers tried to stop my truck an shot at me an like to have kilt me when I was headed to Nashville one night with a load of shine...I said to hell with this, I’m goin into a new line of work. So I said a prayer an left the hills an tha Lord directed me to my callin.”

“He was a man of good disposition...I doubt he had a mean bone in his body. I don’t know of him ever hurting a hair on anybody. Stealing cars was just what he did and he did it without hurting anyone and I never heard an ugly word come out of his mouth. I guess he was the best mannered thief I’ve ever known.” I personally heard Chief Rhett tell all this about Road Runner in Daddy’s office. It stuck with me, as did most of the things that were part and parcel of my life with my father, like wrestling matches, boxing bouts, baseball games, going with him at Christmas to deliver bourbon to his customers, raising his fine pack of Beagle hounds and hunting rabbits with him every cold fall and winter.

Before proceeding further with Road Runner’s exploits, some background regarding my father is essential to fully understand the events that occurred on that afternoon when my father captured him. For me, my father was a man far beyond the other fathers I knew. Like Road Runner, he started life poor. He was the oldest son of a proud and funny family who lived in the hills beyond Bordeaux, northwest of Nashville. George Stainback Spain, his father, who we called "Papa" was one-eighth Cherokee; he had olive skin and looked like an Indian; he was a tinsmith, a still maker, whiskey maker and fox hunter; and he never paid one cent of state sales tax which he considered to be illegal. "Mama" Spain was redheaded and the daughter of a wandering Irish tinker. She dipped snuff, had fire in her eyes and laughter and love in her heart. Mama and Papa were as intelligent and funny as any two people I've ever known. And though my father only completed the eighth grade he, like his parents, had a first-class brain and, beyond that, he had world-class ambition to raise himself and his family upward–which he did by being the best car dealer in Nashville. One of the results was that I became the first Spain to graduate from college.

George Joseph Spain, my father, wore expensive suits, fine shoes, oiled his hair close to his scalp, had manicured nails; he could have passed for a professional gangster. Known as "The Cadillac Man" for the fine ones he sold at George Spain Motor Company and those he drove glowed like the diamonds on his fingers. He liked drinking, gambling, boxing and wrestling events, policemen, politicians, lawyers, judges and a fair number of people who lived edgy lives, some of whom were in the numbers racket. When I was five he started taking me to wrestling and boxing matches, and at Christmas, I would proudly ride beside him when he delivered Wild Turkey Bourbon to his best customers and his politician and law enforcement friends. While not especially tall, he was a large man who looked like he could be tough—and he could be! One Saturday night he took me to a "street fighter" boxing match on the top floor of a downtown hotel. In the midst of the shouting, a man sitting behind us began hollering obscenities; instantly, Daddy turned around in his chair and told the man to quit cursing. Then the man made a bad mistake, he told my father to, "Go to Hell!" With that, Daddy jumped up; turned and grabbed the man by his jacket; yanked him to his feet; pressed his fist tight into the man's cheek; and slowly, in one clear word at a time, he said, "If you curse once more I'm going to bust your face up so bad no one's going to know who you are...you got that?" The man's eyes got big; he nodded rapidly and was shoved back into his seat. I don't remember a thing about the boxing match but every detail of what my father said and did I see and hear seventy years later. Yes, he could be tough, but it was his courtesy, his thoughtfulness toward others, his love and care for his family that marked him and made him the good man he was.

Now, on to my father's capture of Road Runner Rigsby. It was a hot, early afternoon in July 1961; I was at my father's car lot to pick up a 1957 red and white Chevrolet station wagon. He had gotten it for me from a black undertaker on a trade-in. Joe and Parks, two black men who worked for my father had it shining like new and filled with gas. My father and I were in his office signing some papers when there was a loud roaring of a car motor and shouting from Joe and Parks. Through the office's plate glass window we could see my car just starting to move as Joe ran up to the driver's door brandishing a broom in one hand and a crowbar in the other while Parks was on the other side whirling a hammer above his head, both yelling to wake the dead. It was like watching a movie in slow motion: Joe–tall and strong–leaning forward, thrusting the broom handle like a spear through the driver's open window and on through the inside of the steering wheel so it couldn't be turned–the car shuddered to a stop.

Then the film sped up: Daddy rushed past me with a pistol in his right hand calling to me, "George Edward, get the handcuffs out of the bottom drawer an bring em to me." The thief was captured without a struggle and brought back inside the office where Daddy pushed him down into a heavy chair and handcuffed him to its arm. Joe and Parks, still gripping their weapons, waited outside, smoking; now and then they looked through the window to see if everything was OK.

While the rest of us were sweating, the thief was calm as a cucumber. He looked at my father and politely asked, "Mr. Spain, I'd be much obliged to you for a smoke." Daddy took a pack of Camels out of his coat pocket, shook a cigarette out, put it in the man's mouth and lit it with his gold lighter. Then he walked around his desk, sat down in his swivel chair and began to silently study the slender, well-mannered man whose dark hair was oiled and slicked downed just like my father's; cleanly shaven and neatly dressed he could have passed for a next-door neighbor. The only thing odd about him was the red and yellow track shoes on his feet. For a long moment no one spoke, then Daddy, who knew who the thief was the second he saw his face, said, "Well, Road Runner, you've sure got yourself in a pickle this time."

He turned to me, "George Edward, meet the famous Road Runner Rigsby, Tennessee's number one car thief and escape artist...Road Runner, meet my son, George Edward Spain."

Road Runner smiled, nodded to me and looked back at Daddy. "Mr. Spain, thanks for the cigarette, Camels are my smokes, too." He took a deep drag on the cigarette, blew three smoke rings and said, "Well, fellows, you caught me dead to rights, sorry there ain't no reward for catchin me...when's the police comin?"

This time the silence was longer. I could see Daddy was thinking. Finally, he said, "No need for any hurry on that; we've got plenty of time. Let's talk a little while. I know a whole lot about you from my police friends and you know what, you and I've got some things in common...we were both born and raised in the hills. You're from a wild and whiskey-making part of Williamson County and I'm from a wild and whiskey-making part of Davidson; I bet you only went as far as the eighth grade; and I bet you had a good mama and daddy, right?"

Road Runner was grinning like a possum, "Well, I'll be doggone, you pretty much got me nailed down...so, and I hope you ain't goin to be offended if I was to ask if your daddy made whiskey like mine?"

And so it began. What an afternoon it turned out to be. Daddy got two glasses and a three-quarters-full bottle of Wild Turkey out of a tall side drawer and poured two tall ones for Road Runner and himself–in those days I didn't drink. He sent Joe and Parks to Brown's Barbecue and got all of us a sandwich and fries. From then on he and Road Runner went to telling one story after another, laughing and slapping their thighs; you could tell they were both trying to one-up the other as the bourbon dropped lower and lower in the bottle until it was gone. As the day wore on it began to grow dark outside and I started to think Daddy was going to invite Road Runner home for supper when the phone rang. The moment my father picked up the phone and said, "Hello, this is George Spain," the smile left his face and in a subdued tone, "Oh, hi honey...I'm just about to leave...George Edward is here and we're finishing up on his...ok...ok...we'll be home in a minute." He hung up and looked at Road Runner, "Well, old Buddy, all good things must come to an end." He opened the bottom drawer, pulled out some keys, stood up, came around the desk, bent down and unlocked the handcuff on Road Runner's wrist. He reached in his coat and got the pack of Camels out and handed them to Road Runner, "Keep em...you know it crossed my mind when we were talking; a little more, one way or the other, I could've been you and you could've been me...so, my friend, go and steal no more...at least, not from me...let's go outside, I want to watch you run."

I swear, when we stepped outside and the lot's bright lights hit Road Runner's face, I saw his eyes glistening, like when tears are in them. He took my father's right hand in both of his, held it for a moment, then let it go and spun around like a top in his red and yellow track shoes, and in two strides he disappeared!

Three days before Christmas that year, Daddy got a letter from the Williamson County Jail. It was from Road Runner. It read, "Well, they finally got me, Mr. Spain. Two highway patrol officers on motorcycles caught me in a big cow pasture when I slipped on a patty and went down. I hope this finds you and your family well and wish all of you a Merry Christmas. When I get out I plan to come by and bring you a fresh pack of Camels. Mr. Spain, if ever I was to buy a car I'd sure enough buy it from you but, as you know, all kinds of folks just keep on letting me have theirs free. Tell George Edward that his friend, Road Runner, said, 'Hi'."

...of the unusual people I've met in life...

or in my brain...

John Gaunt
Lucy Taggert
Lafe
The Spirit
Cracked
Around the Court House
White Man's Burden Blues

John Gaunt

John Beaufort Gaunt, the High Sheriff of Franklin County, stuck his tongue out and tasted the air; the rich smells of the late breakfast he had just eaten were thick enough to bite: country ham, fried eggs, fried apples, buttered grits, red-eye gravy, buttermilk biscuits, molasses and three cups of steaming black coffee. He was stuffed.

But not satisfied. Now came the time for the best part of every meal; he reached over with his fork, skewered two of the last three biscuits from the biscuit plate, deposited them onto the food-stained blue-and-white Wedgewood breakfast plate in front of him and began methodically to cut each biscuit into four pieces. When he finished, he lifted the lid from a small yellow porcelain cow, picking it up by the curved tail, tipping its head downward and watched the hot milk gravy pour from the cow's wide mouth until the biscuits were completely covered–his dessert at the end of every meal. But before he scooped up the first spoonful to eat, he reached out and got the last biscuit, dipped one end in the gravy on his plate and said, "Crab, come forth from thy den thou sour-natured beast."

There was a scrabbling sound; from under the table crawled a large ugly brindle hound. He sat up, opened his mouth wide and grabbed the biscuit as it fell through the air. Crab chewed twice, swallowed, licked his lips and opened his mouth again. The Sheriff grinned and shook his finger in the dog's face, then pointed to the open doorway to the entrance hall and, with feigned sternness, commanded, "Get thee ta a nunnery, thou breeder of sinners, an wait there for me." The dog padded out the door and disappeared toward the front door where he lay down to await his master's departure.

John Gaunt turned slightly in his chair and looked out the window. He thought, *My God, why didst thou promise such a beauteous day?* He shook his head and spoke aloud to himself, "That po boy, what was his first thought when he woke up this mornin?" From his vest pocket, he pulled out the gold watch Jinny had given him on his fiftieth birthday, snapped the lid open and looked at the hour hand. *Good! There's no need ta hurry, there's plenty of time.*

He frowned, sucked on his teeth three times, pried with his tongue, but failed to dislodge the piece of ham gristle stuck between his gum and right eyetooth. *Damn it!* With the long, sharp fingernail on the little finger of his left hand, he picked at the gristle until finally it came loose, examined it, licked it off, chewed a few seconds, swallowed and smiled - *Now, ta tha ambrosia of tha gods.*

As he ate the biscuits and gravy, his six-foot-six, three-hundred-thirty-pound body sat comfortably upon a well padded, high-back walnut chair made as a gift by one of his former slaves, just for him—the largest man in Franklin County. The chair dwarfed the other thirteen that lined the shining fourteenth-century oak refectory table, his grandfather said had come from the Warwickshire castle of their ancestor, John of Gaunt, 1st Duke of Lancaster.

He was proud of his blood. An oil painting of the Lancaster coat of arms—a shield of red, blue, white and gold with lions and castles—hung above the fireplace in the library. Locked in his highboy desk was the Crown's original land grant that brought his great grandfather, John Edward Gaunt, from England to Virginia. Beneath the document was another, signed by his grandfather, John Henry Gaunt, for the purchase of four thousand acres that he, his wife and five children with seven ox-drawn wagons and twenty-nine slaves traveled a month to reach; a long, hard trip from Virginia, across the Appalachians, through miles and miles of forests, over rivers eventually to Franklin County; to the land that was to make them wealthy. Now, he, John Beaufort Gaunt, owned the land; it stretched from the lower slopes of the Cumberland Plateau to the Elk River. One day it would all go to his son and daughter.

Propped up at a slant on the other side of the breakfast plate was a small leather-bound copy of Shakespeare's Complete Sonnets. The Sheriff was trying to memorize all of them. Number 34, the one before him, was his favorite:

Why didst thou promise such a beauteous day,
An make me travel forth without my cloak,
Ta let base clouds o'ertake me in my way,
Hidin thy bravery in their rotten smoke?
'Tis not enough that through tha cloud thou break,
Ta dry tha rain on my storm-beaten face,
Fo no man...Fo no man...Fo no man...

"Goddamn it ta hell! Goddamn it...what in hell goes after 'no man'?"

As the words came from his mouth he heard quick footfalls and her first words before the kitchen door opened, "John Beaufort, you hush up that kind of ugly talk right now; you're talkin loud enough for everyone ta hear you all tha way down ta tha Courthouse!" A scowl was on Virginia "Jinny" Randolph Gaunt's face as she marched into the dining room, shaking her finger at her husband. "Can you imagine your grandchildren hearin you talk thata way? An you promised me you'd quit cussin in tha house."

He looked down at the last three bites of the biscuits and gravy and wished he'd been eating instead of reciting and cursing, "I know, I know. I'm sorry. But dad-blast it, when I get mad I forget...an I've got that thing on my mind I've got ta take care of at noon."

"Well, you remember who you are, an where you came from, an who your people are, an who I am!" With that, she walked over and kissed him on the bald spot on top of his head, turned and went back through the open doorway. As she closed the door behind her she said, "At least, you got a pretty day."

"O, Jinny, come back just a minute, please."

The door opened, "Yes?" she asked.

"Did ya save some fer me ta take ta tha boy?"

"I'll have his an your lunch an somethin for tha twins ready by tha time you light your cigar. I've got him two ham an biscuits, two fried peach pies an a jar of milk."

"That'll do."

She turned back, leaving the kitchen and closed the door.

At fifty-three, Jinny Gaunt was still a superb looking woman. While none of the Randolph women were parlor room beauties, back in Virginia and now in Tennessee, they were known as 'striking' with their high cheekbones, intelligent eyes, long necks, tall, slender figures, good posture and good manners. Jinny had all of these and more: She was a hard worker, a good cook, a good mother and the love of her husband's life.

He made people uneasy, however; many avoided his eyes when they met him on the street or in the Courthouse. Even at church he was an uncomfortable presence; no one, other than his family, wanted to sit in the same pew with him. It wasn't just his bigness; his face was a threat; two inches above his right eyebrow a purple, half-moon scar half the size of a silver dollar stared at the starer. The scar kept his eyebrow permanently raised above an eye that never seemed to blink.

His eyes, face, size and his reputation belied his tenderness with Jinny and their children and grandchildren who worshiped him and his elegant neatness and good taste for the finer things in life. None of these things gave a hint of his war years: sleeping on the ground; going without bathing for weeks, filthy, unshaven; burned by the sun; soaked by rain; chased and hunted through the mountains; living more like an animal than a human, killing and burning and killing over and over.

Now, he bathed daily, sometimes twice in the dead of summer; he trimmed his short beard a little every morning; his clothes, shoes, boots, books, horses, buggy and guns were the best to be bought, most from England.

Few, if any in the county, were deceived by these fine qualities; they all knew who he had been and who he was now: a Confederate bushwhacker, a terror to all; and now, he was both the High Sheriff and head of the local Klan. During the last three years of the war, he'd tortured, burned and killed both Yankees and civilians—men, women and boys, colored and white, and animals of every kind. When he was elected Sheriff in 1867 and Grand Cyclops that same year, he kept on killing, some legally, some for the sake of the justice he believed was needed to bring an end to the chaos that was destroying all he loved; if he did not punish the evil ones who were tearing apart what little beauty and order that remained, then the South would be lost forever. The people of Franklin County knew that he had once killed children with their parents in a fire; yet they voted for him because he gave them order, order they had prayed for through the long years of evil and violence. And so they were quiet and reelected him over and over again.

It was said that he had killed thirty-seven people. He did not dispute it.

John Gaunt poured the last of the gravy onto the plate, lifted the plate with both hands, bent his head down and licked and licked until the plate looked as clean as if it had just been washed. He set it down, laid the knife and fork side by side upon it, pulled off his napkin, folded it neatly and placed it beside the plate. From inside his vest pocket he took out a cigar and box of matches, put the cigar in his mouth, took a match from the box, flicked it with his thumbnail, lit the cigar and drew deeply on it three times, leaned his head back and blew a cloud of smoke upward through the long, curved arms of his wife's grandfather's gold and crystal chandelier. He was full and he was comfortable. As he studied the rising smoke, each word of the last part of Number 34 came to him, each one in its place, each one down to the last word:

Fo no man well of such a salve can speak
That heals tha wound, an cures not tha disgrace:
Nor can thy shame give physic to my grief;

Though thou repent, yet I have still tha loss:
Tha offender's sorrow lends but weak relief
Ta him that bears tha strong offence's cross.
Ah, but those tears are pearl which thy love sheeds,
An they are rich, an ransom all ill deeds.

My God, that man could write, 'Tha offender's sorrow lends but weak relief ta him that bears tha strong offence's cross. Ah, but those tears are pearl which thy love sheeds, an are rich, an ransom all ill deeds.' Damn, that's better than tha Bible.

With inferiors and those who followed him in the war and in the Klan—some who could not read or write their names—John Gaunt changed his language and manner; he became blasphemous, harsh, direct and short with his words; his speech so like theirs they believed he was one of them, and believing that, they more readily obeyed his will.

In truth, he was an educated man, a highly educated man: two years at Harvard, a year reading law with John Bell and in his Winchester home with its twelve-foot ceilings, the library had wall-to-wall shelves that held the largest and finest collection of books between Nashville and Montgomery.

He licked his lips. Looked at his watch; it was almost time.

He closed the book, picked it up and scooted his chair back, stood up, walked to the kitchen door, opened it and walked in. Jinny was sitting at the kitchen table mixing dough. She had her apron on; her long, dark-brown hair was tied up in a bun, white flour covered her hands and forearms. She pointed with her elbow, "Ya'lls food's in tha lunch pail with a cloth over it." She held up her face and pursed her lips, "Kiss me, Mr. Gaunt."

"Yes, ma'am," he kissed her.

"An comfort that boy all you can."

"I'll try. Why in tha devil did he have ta go an..." he looked over at the wall clock. "Well, it's getting time, I'd better get on." He picked up the bucket. "I'll be back fer supper." He went out the other door into the hall. Crab heard his heavy tread and was standing by the front door, wagging his tail, waiting to go.

"You ready ta go? Hold on a minute, an let me pretty myself an get all my stuff on."

He set the pail down, laid the book on top of it, stepped over to the hall tree, lifted his gun belt and holster with its double-barrel revolver off a peg, buckled the belt around his waist, then took his black frock coat down, dusted a bit of lint off the right lapel, put the coat on, patted the right pocket to be sure the derringer was there, then patted the left one and felt the knife. He looked in the hall tree's mirror, straightened the bow tie, smoothed down his short-cut oiled hair, took his black wide-brimmed felt hat off a peg and put it on his head, straight and secure.

Now, he was ready to face the world. He picked up the book, put it inside the coat's breast pocket, then lifted the pail by its handle, opened the door, stepped outside and closed the door behind him and Crab.

It was a bright, early autumn day; the black-eyed Susans were in full bloom; the deep green was just starting to fade from the two old maples in the front yard; the air was fresh with the hint of a nip in it. Crab followed beside his master's right boot heel as they walked across the broad porch with its six square white columns; went down the steps, between two large boxwoods, to the brick walkway that led across the yard to the gate of the iron fence that surrounded the house and gardens.

The house was two blocks from the square and courthouse. The fine breakfast and fine weather comforted his thoughts as he walked toward town smoking the cigar, *Yer a lucky man, John Gaunt, ya've got a good wife, a good dog, a good cigar...an Shakespeare, what more can a man ask? 'Why didst thou promise such a beauteous day, And make me travel forth without my cloak, ta let base clouds o'ertake me in my way, hidin thy brav'ry in their rotten smoke?'* He smiled, took another puff on the cigar, blew the smoke out and pondered the Bard's words.

As they neared the square he stopped and looked down at the dog, which had immediately sat back on his haunches and looked up at him. "Well, Crab, what do ya think? Is this, or is this not a beauteous day?" Crab tilted his head and looked at the pail, then up at his master, then back at the pail.

"Crab, ya don't give a good goddamn about Shakespeare, do ya? You don't even care that he named ya. You're just a damn beggar, a sour-natured beggar." He set the pail down and pulled back the cloth. "Well, hell, that boy probably won't touch any of it...an I'm sure one of these'll be more than enough." As he talked to the dog, he unwrapped the two fried pies, took one, wrapping the other, put it back in the pail and covered it with the cloth. Holding the pie out in front of him, he said, "Well, ask for it."

With one, quick, sharp bark, Crab caught the falling pie in the air, and it was gone.

It was Saturday: the wagons, buggies, mules and horses of the farmers and sharecroppers, white and Negro, surrounded the courthouse. Beneath an ancient maple, a dozen men sat on benches in a circle; two of them, each with a leg gone, had crutches; another had no right arm; another with a face half gone: parts taken from them at Shiloh, Stones River, Franklin, Nashville, Kennesaw. Some were smoking pipes, others whittling, talking, now and then laughing loudly, chewing, spitting, re-fighting battles and remembering the dead. Little boys—some sons, some grandsons, others just boys—crowded around the men, so near them, they could smell the gunpowder, smoke and blood; hear the roar of cannons, the tearing crash of rifles, explosions, horses whinnying, men shouting and screaming; for a bit they were men themselves, standing with their guns ready to fire, standing shoulder to shoulder beside their heroes. What they heard they never forgot.

Two nods to the Sheriff as he passed. No word was spoken between them—most looked down.

He walked on, Crab at his heels, to the other side of the square where he turned down a short street to a two-story brick building that stood alone on the bank, high above the river. Over the door of the building was a gray sign with dark green letters that read, "Franklin County Jail."

He stopped in front of the building, opened his watch and looked down; both the big hand and little hand stood straight up. It was time. His sister's twins, both his deputies, stood smoking on the front porch. The wagon was waiting. The Negro driver sat like an ebony statue. He wore a black suit and a high-collared white shirt and black string tie. His face showed no emotion. He was looking straight ahead. Brother Joseph Myron, minister of the Winchester Baptist Church, holding his Bible open, stood on the porch shifting his weight back and forth, wishing he was elsewhere; his lips were moving, but the words were silent. The Sheriff nodded to the twins, "It's time." They turned and went inside.

* * * * * * *

The boy sits rigidly upright just as his mother had taught him to sit when he was in church or at home when company came. His ankles and wrists are shackled with heavy chains, he sits in one of two ladder-back chairs that face backward in the bed of the wagon, Brother Myron sits in the other. Beneath the chairs is a rolled-up blanket. Crab sits on the wagon seat between the Sheriff and the Negro. The lunch pail is on the floor in front of Crab. Mounted on their matching grays, the twins follow four strides behind the wagon.

The wagon's movements are as slow and comfortable and steady as a rocking chair. The road's ruts have recently been leveled and filled in before the coming of the winter rains. A brief early morning shower has settled the dust. The air is clear and clean; it comes easy into the lungs. Sounds carry long distances from the river a hundred yards away, a kingfisher's rattling crackles; on the far side of the river, a crow caws from the field where dried shocks of corn stand like small tents in a village; a quail whistles nearby, another answers.

The backs of the Sheriff and the Negro almost touch those of Brother Myron and the boy. Crab has turned completely around on the wagon seat and is sniffing the greasy, rust-red hair and dirty neck of the boy. The boy, like the Negro, does not move or speak.

Jack Garner, the boy, is from Sherwood, a village near the south slope of Sewanee Mountain. He is sixteen, barely over five feet tall, sinewy and dangerous. Three months of hiding in Buggy Top Cave and two months locked in the county jail have turned his face and hands grayish-white. His flint-gray eyes have no light; they register little difference in what they see, whether human or stone. He cannot read or write but he can kill with no more remorse than wringing a chicken's neck or hammering a hog's head. He has killed seven people.

"Jack?" asks the Sheriff.

He does not answer.

The Sheriff turns his head sideways toward the boy.

"Jack, ya hear me?"

For a moment there's no answer then, "Yes, sir, I hyair." It is spoken without life, as though to no one.

"Jack, ya want a ham an biscuit an a peach pie? Ya still got time."

"Naw, sir, I reckon not. I ain't hongry right now. Maybe later."

"Let me know if ya change yer mind, cause ya ain't got much time. Jack, do ya know Shakespeare?"

"Who?"

"Shakespeare?"

"Naw, sir."

"Well listen ta this."

Though thou repent, yet I have still tha loss:
Tha offender's sorrow lends but weak relief
Ta him that bears tha strong offence's cross.
Ah, but those tears are pearl which thy love sheeds,
An they are rich, an ransom all ill deeds.

"Shakespeare wrote that, Jack...do you know what repent means?"

"Naw, sir, but I member a preacher spoke hit once."

"Well, it means you feel sad about somethin ya done that was bad."

"Yes, sir."

"Like feelin sad about killin ya mama an daddy an yer brothers an sister an burnin tha house down on em...Jack, why'd ya do it?"

"Jus cause."

"Damnit, jus cause why?"

"Cause what they done."

"Well, Jack, what'n hell was that?"

"Thas all I know, hits jus cause what they done."

"Well, then, have ya repented fer doin it?

"Naw, sir, I'm not real sure I feel bad or sad bout doin it."

"Well, I'll be goddamn...scuse me, Brother Myron."

A brown wood thrush flies out of the roadside hedge, crossing just below the mules' eyes; their heads jerk upward; they almost stop moving but do not; they move on steadily but without hurry, pulling the wagon and its four occupants toward their destination; in the dust of the road lies tracks of buggies, wagons, horse and mule hooves, all going toward Lynch Hill.

The Sheriff hacks and spits, "Brother Myron, can't ya say or read somethin that'll help? Hell, he's runnin outta time. Ask im if he's been saved an, if not, does he wanta be. Say somethin...anything."

Brother Myron's body stiffens though he is already sitting as stiff and straight as the chair he is sitting on. He is a young man with light blonde, almost white hair that has begun to thin. His eyes are pale blue. Some think he is an albino but he is not. His mouth seems too small to belong to a preacher. There are large red splotches on both sides of his fair-skin neck. He is terrified of the Sheriff. He opens his mouth and starts to speak but nothing comes out; he swallows, pulls a handkerchief out of the side pocket of his shabby black suit, wipes the sweat off his face and stammers, "Well...well...well, I guess, I guess...I guess, it might be a good time to pray. Let us bow our heads."

All four in the wagon bow their heads. The twins do not. The Sheriff begins to scratch behind Crab's ears. The dog's eyes close with contentment. Brother Myron clears his throat, puts his hand on Jack's shoulder and, in his most sonorous voice of God, begins to pray:

O, *Lawd Gawd Almighty, hear thy servant's prayer. Though tha Devil hath hold of this sinner ah ask thee in thy son's name ta cast tha demon out of im an free im so he can confess his sins an repent an confess thy name as Lawd an be saved rather than die in the depths of his depravity, which he will in just a little bit, as we draw near to where we are goin...*He pauses, turns and looks beyond the mules...*O, Lawd God, we're almost there. Aaaahh-man!*

They raise their heads and open their eyes. The mules' steady forward motion continues at their unhurried pace. As the wagon comes around a bend in the road there is a break in the hedge. For an instant the Sheriff sees the cluster of people, horses, mules, wagons and buggies at the bottom of the distant hill; at its top stands a single tall oak tree. He turns on the wagon seat, looks behind him; Brother Myron is slowly turning the pages in the Bible on his lap. The Sheriff's voice is hard and loud enough to cause the Negro to glance sideways at him, "Damn ya, preacher, hurry up an save im or that boy's goin straight ta hell before tha hour's up...an ya may be goin too if ya don't hurry up!"

Immediately, Brother Myron lays the Bible under the chair, turns and takes hold of Jack's hands and in a voice that is now a mewing plea, "Jack, I beg you ta listen ta me. Time's runnin out, I wanta read something that'll give ya comfort.

Jesus said, I am the resurrection, an tha life; he that believeth in me,

Though he were dead, yet shall he live; an whosoever liveth an

Believeth in me shall never die. Believest thou this?

"Jack, do ya believe that?"

"What's that?"

"Listen to me now, Jack; look inta my eyes; do ya believe in Jesus?"

Jack turned and looked straight into the eyes of the preacher. "Yes, I guess I do, cause my mama raised me ta believe in im."

"Praise Jesus! Jack, say it loud enough for tha Sheriff ta hear ya. Say, 'I believe in Jesus!'"

"I believe in Jesus."

"Praise tha Lawd! Say it louder, Jack."

"PRAISE JESUS!"

"Did ya hear im, Sheriff? Did ya hear im? Do ya want im ta say it agin?"

"Naw, I heard im. That's enough. Preacher, you can be quiet now...ya done good, Jack; ya want a ham an biscuit?"

"Yes, sir, I think I'll take one now."

The Sheriff pulls the cloth off the lunch pail, picks out the larger ham and biscuit and hands it to Jack who takes it in both hands, lifts it to his mouth and, just as he is about to take a bite, the Sheriff says, "Hold on, Jack. Don't ya wanta say a prayer before ya eat."

"Yes, sir, I guess so. I know one my mama taught me."

"Say it, Jack, say it."

"Aw right, I'll try...now I...now I lay me down ta sleep, I pray...I pray tha Lord...I pray tha Lord my soul ta keep. God bless mama an papa an all my brothers an sister. Amen. Did I do alright, Sheriff?"

Except for the muffled sound of the mule's hooves and the creaking of the wagon, there was silence. Then came a quick intake of breath and a barely audible sob from the Negro who had pulled a handkerchief from his coat pocket and was wiping his eyes.

For a long moment the Sheriff says nothing; the muscles in his jaws tighten; his left hand rests on Crab's back, then he says, "Ya did fine, Jack, your mama would've been proud of ya."

The boy eats. The Negro's face is as it was. The Sheriff looks down at the dog, removes his hand and looks toward the crowd of onlookers gathered on the hill. Brother Myron sits straight up. Everyone is quiet. Jack swallows the last bit of the ham and biscuit. The wagon turns off the rode and climbs to the top of the hill under the oak tree where it stops. The rear of the wagon bed is beneath a large limb. From the limb hangs a noose.

Every eye is on the boy and the Sheriff who has risen to his feet. Like a huge bear, he tilts the wagon slightly, as he turns and steps over the back of the seat into the bed.

Crab's eyes follow him. Brother Myron seems confused as to what he is to do; his eyes are fixed on the Sheriff's face for some sign or word to direct him.

"Preacher, make yerself useful; help the boy to his feet...Jack, stand up an let Brother Myron help ya...then I'll take over."

Jack did not rise. He looks at the Sheriff, and in a voice that might have been spoken at the dinner table, he asks, "Sheriff, can I have my peach pie now?"

"What?"

"Can I have my peach pie now, please, sir?"

"Peach pie?"

"Yes, sir."

"Well...well ok, but ya got ta eat up an not keep all these folks waitin."

"Yes, sir."

"Lijah, reach in that pail an give tha boy that peach pie."

"Yah, Suh." The Negro, who is of an indeterminate age, shows neither fear nor the slightest hint of affection in his face or voice for the Sheriff, for whom he has been body servant and buggy driver for twenty years. He removes the cloth, pulls out a pie and hands it to Jack who takes it in both hands and begins to eat, unbothered by the peach juice running down his chin onto his shirt.

The crowd watches. They are silent and still. A saddle mule, tied to the back of a wagon with a sack of seed corn on its back, brays and paws the ground. A breeze ripples waves across the grass on the hill, bare of trees but for the oak at the very top.

The Sheriff looks at the crowd, turns his head, and nods at the boy, then looks back at the crowd, "Ya'll just have ta be patient." He walks to the rear of the wagon, reaches up and adjusts the noose, opening it wider, then turns back to Jack who has finished the pie.

"OK, Jack, it's time, get on ya feet! Preacher, help im up."

Brother Myron steps toward Jack, grasps his forearms and as gently as he can, pulls the boy to his feet; the clanking of the shackles is the only sound heard. The preacher's face is as if in a dream as he slips to the side of the boy and with his arm around his waist guides him almost to the end of the wagon.

The Sheriff studies the preacher's face for a moment and shakes his head, "Preacher, yer just about worthless, ain't ya...well, don't just stand there lookin at me, find something to read that'll be a comfort."

Brother Myron steps back, bends over and gets his Bible, opens it to where he had placed a ribbon and begins to read in a new voice, one that is natural and gentle and kind:

The Lord is my Shepherd; I'll not want. He maketh me to lie down in green pastures: he leadeth me beside the still waters. He restoreth my soul: he leadeth me in the paths of righteousness for his name's sake. Yea, though I walk through the valley of the shadow of death, I will fear no evil: for thou art with me; thy rod and thy staff they comfort me. Thou preparest a table before me in the presence of mine enemies; thou anointest my head with oil; my cup runneth over. Surely goodness and mercy shall follow me all the days of my life; and I will dwell in the house of the Lord forever.

When the Bible reading ends, the Sheriff drags the boy's chair to the rear, lets the tailgate down, and places the chair at the edge of the wagon bed. He reaches up, pulls the noose down, placing the loop over the boy's head and easing it down onto his neck, tightens it so that the knot is behind the left ear.

"Jack, step up on the chair."

"Yes, sir, but I'll need some help."

"I'll lift ya." He reaches around the boy's waist and raises him until he is standing on the seat of the chair.

Jack's face is only inches from the Sheriff's. "Are ya gonna hang me now?" he asked.

"Yeh, Jack, I'm gonna hang ya now."

"Ya ain't mad at me, are ya?"

"No, Jack, I ain't mad at ya."

"Thas good."

Lijah is watching over his shoulder; waiting for the signal. Crab watches also, as though he too is waiting for the signal. Brother Myron stares at the boy; his mouth opens and shuts, over and over, and not a word or sound comes out. The twins back their horses away from the rear of the wagon.

"Will it hurt?" asks Jack.

"Naw, Jack, you won't feel a thing." The Sheriff points to a distant church steeple. "Look, Jack...look way off there. Can ya see that church steeple in Winchester?" As he speaks he eases backwards to the front of the wagon bed, sits down in the preacher's chair and whispers, *"Now, Lijah!"*

"HAH!" shouts Lijah and slaps the reins hard. The mules jerk the wagon forward.

"Yes, sir," says Jack, "I think I..." and falls into the air.

Lucy Taggert's Six Letters

Those who love in excess also hate in excess.

Aristotle

My Lord, Lucy Gaunt Taggert was a stunningly beautiful woman! Every small bit of her body, every small bit of her mind and soul and all of her spirit was a woman's—a woman second to none and certainly second to no man.

Her long, straight neck was crowned by a finely shaped head with a face so strong and striking that men, and even women, could not help but stare at her. Her head was always held high with her slightly curly, soft-gray hair drawn tightly back in a bun. Her face toned with pride; her eyes, ash-colored, intelligent, reserved, almost cold, seldom blinked as they saw the lies and fears beneath the masks of others; her lips, full and pink, pursed slightly as might a young woman who was about to kiss her lover. She was sixty-three....

Her beauty was sensual, not like that of a rose or a sunset, it was the beauty of the bed; her flesh, touched with light and shadows, spread over her body like smooth, white milk. Men sought her but never once did she seek them. Many men, including even her minister, Reverend Thomas Dark of the Estill Springs Baptist Church, could barely control the lust in their faces or voices when they were near her. She treated these men, even if they were among the gentry, with the same coldness she might use when dealing with ill-mannered white trash. When she saw sex in the eyes of Reverend Dark the day he came to her house to comfort and pray with her after Bob's death, she told him to take his Bible and hat and go home and go to bed with his own wife. After that, she never set foot in church again. Men saw her beauty, her aloofness, her perseverance; what they did not see was her anger, an anger that eventually turned into hatred when death came to her home.

In Franklin County, the Gaunts were first among firsts. Raised in wealth and privilege with books, music, art, fine clothes and love of family, Lucy believed as her parents and ministers had taught her to believe: the Bible was the literal word of God and made it absolutely clear that white people were to rule the world and Negroes were to be their servants, their workers in the fields and the cleaners of their chamber pots.

The only man she had ever loved was Robert Taggert; her handsome husband and successful owner of "Jerusalem", a thousand-acre plantation that spread along both sides of Elk River near the village of Estill Springs. He was a good husband and a loving father to their sons Bob, Sam, Hubert and their daughter, Emma.

Then war came. In the late morning of April 27, 1861, Robert and Bob rode into Winchester and enlisted in the 1st Tennessee.

A week later, after making love that last night before he and Bob were to leave, Robert held Lucy close and promised, "I swear to you and I swear to God, I'll keep Bob safe. It'll be over in no time...I won't let anything happen to him...I swear it." At sunrise, when he and Bob were both mounted, he leaned from the saddle, gave her one last kiss and they galloped down the lane. The last she saw of them was the waving of their hats—and they were gone.

In the bitter years ahead Lucy was borne up by her unyielding will and unfaltering faith that God would assure the South prevailed and that Robert and Bob would return safely. Her determination far exceeded Robert's, exceeding even that of her proud and powerful brother, John Gaunt, who led Confederate bushwhackers during the war, and afterward became High Sheriff of Franklin County and Grand Titan of the Ku Klux Klan.

****

On a stifling hot morning at Kennesaw Mountain, Georgia, June 27, 1864, a solid round shot, fired from a Federal battery, tore Lucy's and Robert's lives apart as it ripped away most of the lower part of Robert's left arm then passed on through Bob's head, killing him instantly. More skeleton than man, he rode beside the wagon that carried Bob's coffin; he rode on Bob's mare, Lady, the reins gripped in his right hand, his left sleeve pinned to the shoulder. And so it was in September that when Robert–himself dead inside with guilt–returned home without an arm, he turned away from Lucy who needed him and turned rather into himself and to alcohol, giving her no comfort, showing her no love, much less being a comfort to their twin sons and daughter. Feeling sorrow only for himself he blamed himself for being alive instead of Bob–whom he had loved maybe even more than he had Lucy.

Robert returned to a wife who, though she had yearned for him at night for three long years, had not given way to despair, nor to men who sought her, nor to prayer or God; she did not have time for any of them. Every day from dawn to dark, she worked alongside her sons and daughter and the Negroes in the fields, plowing, planting, chopping; and when the Yankees came and freed the Negroes, she worked all the harder with those few who stayed. Day after day, the sun turning her black until from a distance, she was just one more Negro; she drove them all, the Negroes, her sons, her daughter, herself, harder than any slave driver had ever driven any slave at Jerusalem.

And after all that longing; after all that giving up of who she once had been; after making herself into an animal so that he, Robert, and their remaining children, and she could have something that remained from all that once had been—though nothing could ever be again as it had been, for Bob would never be there with them again—still, after all of that, she had not been dragged down to nothingness.

How can any man fully know the pain of a woman who has lost a child to death? She has felt her child move inside her; her eyes have looked down into her baby's as he suckled; and she has felt his arms around her neck and heard him first say, "Mama;" and then, years later learns her child now a man, has been killed in battle far from home; how can that pain ever fully leave her, knowing she will never see him again, never kiss his cheek? No man, not even a father, can know this pain. She wrote her sister:

Jerusalem – Estill Springs
Thursday, July 7th, 1864

My Dearest Sister Emily,

Word arrived yesterday that our precious Bob is no more. He was killed by the Yankees ten days ago, bravely defending our country at a place called Kennesaw Mountain in Georgia. Robert was struck by the same shell and is badly wounded. He lies near death in a home in Atlanta. May God answer my prayers and save his life. I need him here by my side. Oh, how I need him.

I cannot stop seeing our dear boy, our first child. He is here before me as I write, a little baby in my arms; a boy racing everywhere on his pony; a handsome, tall young man dressed in his new uniform, standing so proudly beside his father; stepping toward me, telling me not to fear, no harm will come to him. And then I hear, again and again, Robert's last words, "I swear to you and I swear to God, I'll keep Bob safe."

Last night, as I got into bed and was about to blow out the candle, I saw him standing just at the edge of the light and distinctly heard his voice say, "I love you." When I lifted my arms toward him he disappeared. Immediately, this morning as I awoke, the sharp coldness that never goes away was in my heart.

Sister, I feel far away from everything; it is all I can do to hold this pen in hand for I am so weakened by the loss of Bob and the fear his father will also depart forever from me. But as in all things, whatever our dear Savior chooses for our suffering, all we as His people can say is, "Praise thee, Lord God, our creator and redeemer."

Without God's hands holding me up I do not know if I could go on; every decision is upon me, I grow angrier and angrier at having to urge the children and Negroes to work. At times, even hatred fills me against those from the North who have brought death and destruction to our Southern people. What the Yankees have not stolen from Jerusalem the Negroes have. Half or more of the field hands have left with what they could take and those who remain are old or nearly useless—of the house servants only Aunt Sally remains.

Truly, I have no time to grieve. It seems every moment is taken in seeing that my little ones have food to eat and clothes to wear. I work in the fields with the boys and Negroes from dark to dark. More and more, I am looking and smelling like a Negro. The sun has turned me black. If you saw me from a distance you could not tell the difference between me and one of the "niggers". At times, I wonder if I am becoming one of them. I go for days without bathing or combing my hair, most of the time it is tangled just like theirs. Other than my family and the land, I have grown to care little for anyone. I once was a good "Rebel" but now I hate the word and hate those who led us into this war, most especially do I hate the Yankees. I pray my heart is not so seared with bitterness that I will never be capable of caring for others as I once did.

Emily, it is my prayer that your children, all our children never suffer what we have suffered, never hate as I hate. Will our God forgive me for the hatred I have because of the death of my baby boy and the terrible deformation that is Robert's? My dear sister, pray for us.

Brother is still in the mountains. What he and his men have lived through I cannot imagine but it makes me love him the more. They have done all they can to protect us from the hordes of Yankees that have descended upon us and driven him south of the mountains so that we are alone but for God. But as Paul's glorious words declared, "If God be for us who can stand against us?" May God protect our brave brother and his men as the end draws near for these terrible times.

It has been a year since your dear husband John and his brother were captured. What word do you hear from him of their condition? A year has passed since Gettysburg and all I know from you is that they are in a large prison somewhere in Maryland. But you and I know, dearest Emily, the Lord's wings are spread wide and are protecting them.

Tell sweet Bonnie and Stewart that "Auntie" Lucy sends hugs and kisses and wishes that we shall all be together soon, and when we are I will bake them my special sweet potato pie they love so much. Good night, my precious sister, and know, as do I, that our Heavenly Father watches over us and in His own good time will unite us again–and most especially you with your beloved John.

Your loving sister,
Lucy

Jerusalem - Estill Springs
Friday, July 29th, 1864

Dearest Sister Emily,

Our Lord and Savior be praised, Robert is home and in his bed where I shall nurse him night and day until he is well again. Last week, a Mr. Arthur Hammond, an elderly gentleman, a native of Atlanta and owner of the home where Robert has lived since he was wounded, brought Bob's body back in a pine coffin with my poor Robert riding Bob's horse all those long miles beside the wagon. I offered Mr. Hammond what little money we had but he would not take it, saying, "Mrs. Taggert, you have given a son for us, your husband has given an arm, you have paid many times over. God bless you!"

We buried our gentle Bob today in the plot Brother purchased for the family in the Winchester City Cemetery.

Oh, Emily, even with all the cruelty, there are still good people in the world which is of some comfort. As is everyone, we know we are poor, usually there is only enough food for us and the Negroes to survive. Grain is very high and hardly can be bought. Sometimes the children come to me and beg for food, saying over and over, "Mama, we're so hungry...Mama, we're so hungry." We are left with only a few half-wild hogs, a handful of chickens that rarely lay and two bony mules that Uncle Henry kept hidden in the cane. Where we used to give away our old clothes to the poor, now I mend them and we keep wearing them until they are only good for rags.

But, thank God, I still have my precious Robert and our fine boys, Sam and Hubert and our pretty little Emma. Robert's wound has no darkness or odor as occurs with moldering; I keep it clean and greased and put on fresh dressings every day. He is so brave. He never groans when I wash his wound or massage and exercise his upper arm. My only worry is that he seldom smiles and then only for an instant. He rarely initiates conversation and seems totally uninterested in what is occurring with the crops and what little livestock we have left. Mostly, he sits alone in his library with maybe an open book on his lap that he does not look down on; rather he seems to be staring into the distance; and when I ask him, "Robert, what is it, what are you thinking?" he continues to stare for a moment, then he looks up at me almost as though he doesn't recognize me. He might just shake his head or say, "Oh nothing...nothing at all." He hardly eats a bite and I am beginning to worry for his want of whiskey, which he has Uncle Henry get from a Negro who makes it. I pray for him nightly that our God who can do all things, will bring healing, not only to his body but equally to his mind and soul.

At times, I am nearly overwhelmed with guilt because I have so little time for the children. When I am with them I am so tired I can barely speak or smile when they tell me something or show me something they have made. Our good Aunt Sally is with them more than I. They seem to love her and I truly believe she loves them, but she is not their mother—I am! The older they get the more I expect of them. When I have them working in the fields, I yell at them the same as I yell at the Negroes. When we are there in the fields I am the driver: I expect them to hoe, chop, pick whatever is there to pick: cotton, corn, melons, beans, whatever there is that needs picking, and then I expect them to haul it away. But at night, as I lie in bed, I sometimes see them again in my arms, I see my babies and I fall asleep happy; then, come morning, when it is time to return to the fields, I am their driver again—as I must be if we are to survive!

Yesterday evening, just before the light began to fade, there was a pounding of hooves up the lane, across the front yard, then into the back and on toward the barn. It was another gang of cursed Yankees. They carried off the last two hams in the smokehouse; they found the salt, sugar, eggs and syrup hidden under the hay in the loft. I had had all I could stand of their thievery and did not care if they rode me down or shot me. I ran out the back door and shouted at them to get off our land and leave us alone. With that, four of them began riding in circles around me, laughing, almost knocking me to the ground, cursing, saying they would do what they damned well pleased and they would be where they damned well pleased and no "Rebel b---h" was going to tell them what to do and that if I did not shut up and go back inside, they would burn the house and barns and quarters to the ground. Finally, I went back inside, but Emily, I swear if I had had a gun I would have done my best to kill them all. Later when it was dark, a few more came and carried off what turkeys and chickens they could find. May Abraham Lincoln die and his soul burn in hell for what he has done to us.

Forgive me, sister, for unburdening all my anger and worries on you, as you have your own burdens to bear in these dark days. I so wish we were nearer one another as I miss your comforting voice and gentle smile. I suppose the Yankees have spread like locusts through southern Kentucky the same as they have throughout Tennessee. When will our armies strike a blow and drive them away? If it is not done soon I fear for the future of our Confederacy.

You will remember Ella Randolph; she is to be confined soon until her baby comes. As you know, her constitution is not strong. Poor thing, she has already lost two babies. I pray the Lord will see fit for her to keep this one.

I suppose that is all I have to say for now. Please write me back soon and tell me all the happy things you remember of Papa and Mama and our joyful days of childhood. I fear my prayers sometimes seek revenge yet I know the Lord's will prevails in all things and that His grace and forgiveness can extend even to the evil that is sometimes in my heart. I send my love to all of you.

Your loving sister,

Lucy

****

In the spring of 1865 the Confederacy surrendered. The Civil War was over. The South was in ruins. Three hundred thousand Confederates had been killed. Four million slaves were free. Fields that had grown cotton, corn and wheat returned to weeds and forests. Houses, barns, gins, mills and fences had been burned. Cattle, hogs, sheep, horses, mules and chickens had been killed or taken by the passing armies. Hunger, even starvation, was spread across the land. Mothers were without milk in their breasts. Babies died. The eyes of the men who had seen their friends killed and maimed and who had killed their enemy with Minie ball and bayonet, stared far off seeing something somewhere else.

Little money was to be had. The yoke of Reconstruction lay heavy on the neck of the South. Four years of killing and suffering had made people hard. Distrust of neighbors, at times, even cruelty toward them became easy. Away from the large cities there was little to no law. Secret vigilantes rose up; the largest, the Ku Klux Klan, rode at night to whip and hang and burn the immoral, the wrongdoer and any Negro who offended or threatened white men and, most especially, white women. With the destruction of their way of life many white southerners surrendered to fear and hopelessness. Some did not. Lucy Taggert never did.

Jerusalem – Estill Springs
Monday, October 17th, 1870

Dearest Emily,

I hope this finds you and your beautiful family well. God be praised, Jerusalem is saved! Prices on last year's and this year's cotton have been enough to pay off our note at the bank and left much to spare. A great load has been lifted off me and now I can begin to think of improvements I have dreamed about. We need a new herd bull and two more rams for our growing flock.

Sharecropping with the Negroes is, to my mind, the best way to get something out of them since we can no longer use the whip. I provide the land, seed, fertilizer and housing and get half the crop. I say, "I" since Robert stays indisposed and leaves the running of Jerusalem entirely to me. Our corn and wheat have also done well as have the cattle, sheep and hogs. We are gradually getting the place back in the order it was before the war. The house, barns, outbuildings, Negroes' houses, fences, fields and woodlots are all in better than middlin' condition. With the coming of cooler weather we have started killing hogs and already have a fair amount of meat in the smokehouse. All in all, we are blessed as compared to many who may never recover from the Yankees' devastation of their property and fortunes. But as in all things, we do not lose faith in Him who has given us His son and our lives.

Without Aunt Sally I do not know what would have become of us. For such a tiny being she does the work of any four other Negroes. She does all the cooking, washing, ironing, house cleaning, making of the fires in winter and has done her best to keep the children in line, though with the boys I am not sure she will succeed as they are strong willed, much like Brother, and say, "No nigger is going to give us orders." Aunt Sally's eyes are red as blood from using red oak bark and alum when she washes our clothes and sheets, which is an almost constant job in itself, but she seems as chipper as ever and her pipe never seems to leave her mouth. She sends her blessing to you and all of your family.

Brother remains tenacious in protecting the county. He has pretty much silenced the mouths of those who stir up everyone by preaching equality for the Negroes. He has driven several of the malcontents out of the county. Recently, he brought to their rightful ends a gang of three road thieves that had been robbing travelers between here and Chattanooga for the better part of a year. He caught them red-handed in the act of robbing a local, highly respected couple, the Johnsons, you may remember them; he runs the bank in Winchester. They were halfway up the mountain heading to Sewanee to visit their son who is a student at the University when Brother caught the thieves in the act of taking the Johnsons' money and rings. He hung them on the spot. The week after that there was a trial of a sixteen-year-old boy from Sherwood who had killed all five of his family and two others. I've enclosed a long newspaper article about the killings and the trial. The jury found the boy guilty and the judge ordered him to be hung. Brother carried out the order two days later but said there was something sad about doing it as the boy was so polite and seemed rather simple and not fully understanding what he had done and what was about to happen to him. I understand that

Brother Myron got him to confess the name of Jesus as Lord before he died.

I am sorry to report that nothing has changed with Robert; if anything, his drinking is worse—with that and eating little, you would hardly know him. About the only time he leaves the house is in the evening when he saddles Bob's mare and goes for a ride, Lord knows where. He rebuffs any suggestions that I or the children try to give to help him.

The weather here has cooled considerably. Though it seems early, I hear there has been some frost already around Sewanee. Hopefully, cold weather will help reduce the fevers that have been so prevalent in our area this summer. If you are through with them, kindly return the candle molds as we need to replenish our stock of candles before winter's darkness sets in.

I thank God for the strength His words give us and for the teachings and good examples of our dear parents. You and I have been blest to be women strong enough to bear many sadnesses; for that strength I know we are both thankful. May it continue until we join the One who is the source of all our strength and of every good and perfect thing.

Forever your loving sister,
Lucy

Jerusalem – Estill Springs
Saturday, April 25th, 1874

My dear sister Emily,

For the first time since Robert returned home I am beginning to feel a glimmer of hope. Several weeks back he agreed to go see a healer woman who Aunt Sally knows and speaks highly of. She says the woman saved her life in childbirth and that of her baby. Robert has always been fond of Aunt Sally and as his drinking has continued without change, she is almost the only one to whom he will speak or listen. Sometime back she talked to 'Mastah Robert' about this healer and finally convinced him to go see her.

The woman's name is Katherine O'Connor. She lives about a mile from the house in a cabin on Elk River with no man; only her boy is there, of whom it is rumored may have some Negro blood. Her reputation as a healer of all sorts of ailments is, according to many, highly regarded. From time to time, I see her on the road walking to Estill; she is comely, has long red hair and always nods politely as we pass.

Tomorrow is Decoration Day. Since the boys are now married and living in Winchester, we only have our sweet Emma still here. She will go with me in the buggy to the cemetery in Winchester where Bob is buried. I wish you could see the nice Gaunt-Taggert family plot Brother has purchased and put an iron fence around. Bob is the only one there for the present but in time all of us will join him. I am expecting as good a crowd as there was last year. Most people bring a lunch basket and when we are finished mowing and weeding and picking up limbs we will begin stuffing ourselves. After Louise Lee reads her poem–she is our county's Poet Laureate and always has one ready for public celebrations–I expect the Episcopal priest, Reverend King, will read a few verses of scripture and offer the blessing. Then, we will dig in. Visiting friends and hearing the latest gossip will be fun. I so wish Robert would go but he says he has an appointment with the healer. Since it seems to be helping, I guess it is best for him to go on. Maybe next year, he will be driving us in the buggy. I think it will do him good to finally visit Bob's grave. He never has.

Oh, my dear sister, may God answer the prayer I have prayed nightly since Robert returned home. May He send His power through this woman so that Robert's mind and soul are healed and he is once again with us and loving us. It seems a lifetime since he has held me in his arms. I need him by my side again to help me with all the many problems there are in operating Jerusalem. Most of all, I need his love. May our loving God grant this.

Love to all your dear family,
Lucy

Jerusalem - Estill Springs
Monday, June 29th, 1874

Dear Emily,

I do not know how to tell you what has happened. I can barely see the words as I write them for the tears in my eyes. Robert is dead. Two nights ago, on the tenth anniversary of Bob's death, he hung himself in Lady's barn stall. Uncle Henry found him. The rope had broken and he was lying in the straw. The horse never stepped on him.

Katherine O'Connor, the healer, is to blame. Brother got it out of Uncle Henry who looked scared and kept whispering to himself. After Brother threatened to whip him if he did not tell everything he knew, he stammered that, "Tha witch conjured Mastah Robert with a love potion." Then Henry began to stammer so he could not be understood. When Brother slapped him, the story poured out. Robert has been going to bed with that woman almost since the first time he went to her cabin. All the niggers on the place knew it and were scared to talk.

I guess this guilt, on top of what he already had about Bob, was just more than Robert could bear so he ended his life. There is no telling what this evil being gave him or said to get him into her bed. Uncle Henry says the boy, who we now know is half nigger, may have helped in some way since Robert had taken a liking to him.

In Exodus twenty-two, verse eighteen there is a command from God which says, "Thou shalt not suffer a witch to live." Last night Brother and the boys and I fulfilled that commandment. The boy got away but we will find him. I know you will not share this with anyone. It may be best to burn this letter after you have read it. We will bury Robert tomorrow beside Bob. Maybe then he can rest in peace. I am sorry this letter is so painful and so brief but I still have much to do.

Lucy

Jerusalem - Estill Springs
Friday, December 20th, 1878

My Dearest Daughter,

God has answered our prayers. Brother finally located Jeremiah, the Negro spawn of Katherine O'Connor, the woman who caused your father to take his own life. He has been living with some people in a valley on the other side of Sewanee. As you remember, he helped his mother make potions with which she bewitched your father and drove him to his death. The boys and I will spend tomorrow night at Brother's in Winchester so we can get an early start in the morning up the mountain. Then we shall see to him.

A long time has gone by since we have written one another, and I am anxious to know that God is dealing kindly with you and that all the little ones are in good health. We wish you could be here with us for Christmas, though we expect little jollification. When I get back home to Jerusalem, I will put this letter in with the other things I am sending and hope you receive it before Christmas or soon thereafter. In the box there is some muslin for you and some dark calico and thread to make dresses for the girls. There is also a nice scrap of black silk that you may find a use for.

The weather here is all gloom and bitter cold. I think it may snow tonight. If not for the hope and confidence that God gives I would be desolate and miserable. It is hard to bear as things grow worse and worse. The war brought great loss and has continued to deprive many; but all praise to our Father, we still have our land.

The price of cotton has fallen so low the boys say we can hardly afford to make a crop next year. Your brothers work hard as there are few Negroes of any account to work. I do not believe the Negro can be elevated to an intelligent and reliable race for their constitution is averse to responsibility. I continue to believe that God created them to be servants but in all things God's will be done. What few of ours that remain with us send their howdies, especially, Uncle Henry and our wonderful Aunt Sally.

Old age is beginning to catch up with Brother. His heart is failing but he will not cut back on eating so he is getting bigger. He is still trying to memorize all of Shakespeare's sonnets. He says it is good for his brain and that he admires Shakespeare above all other writers, I think even more so than King David who was his favorite for many years. As you know he took Crab's name from one of Shakespeare's plays. I swear that is the ugliest dog I have ever seen but the two of them are inseparable. Brother remains the County Sheriff and is doing a good job keeping peace so we never have any trouble with the Negroes. He is still as much a terror to the ungodly as he was during the war. The boys help out as his deputies. I would not be surprised that one of them will take his place when he retires or dies from overeating. God be with him.

You will remember Elisa Capers with whom you were in school. She has lost all three of her children. Both of her precious girls died of the putrid fever last year and three months back she delivered a stillborn baby boy. She has not risen from her bed since then and her flesh has fallen away as she will not eat. I visit her every few days and try to encourage her with good memories of the past and with prayer but to no avail. Her sweet smile we loved so is gone. Yet with all of this, each time I visit she takes my hand and asks about you and the children. Her husband is like an angel as he nurses her but he looks so sad and lost. I fear she will not last out the winter. As in all things, even those as sad as this, may the Lord's will be done.

Enough of unhappy tidings; I want you and my darling grandchildren to begin planning to come down in the spring for a visit and plan to stay a long time because we have much to catch up on. Tell Phillip his mother-in-

law has ordered him to take a rest from lawyering awhile and come with you. I miss all of you. We will have a big party and get as many of your old friends together as are still here. It will be like old times. Bring your newest hats and we will dress up and have Henry drive us everywhere in the buggy. What fun it will be.

I will finish now and get my bag packed for tomorrow. Pray for us that all goes well on the mountain. I will take this with me and may add a bit more about how our business is concluded.

Come in the spring. Love to you and Phillip and kisses for my angels.

Your loving mother

P.S. Last month your daddy and I would have been married 46 years. I still miss him so.

The Home Journal

Winchester, December 23, 1878

Sometime, in the afternoon of Friday, December 21, 1878, John Beaufort Gaunt, High Sheriff of Franklin County Tennessee, his sister, Mrs. Lucy Gaunt Taggert, of Estill Springs and her two sons, Sam and Hubert Taggert, the Sheriff's deputies, both of Winchester, and Lafayette Washington Pearson, a young man from near Sherwood were killed in a bloody shootout on the road between Sewanee and Sherwood. As of this writing, it appears that a sixth person was also involved but as yet the name of that individual is unknown. Services will be conducted tomorrow at 11:00 am by Brother Joseph Myron at the Winchester Baptist Church. Immediately following the service Sheriff Gaunt, Mrs. Taggert, Sam Taggert and Hubert Taggert will be laid to rest in the Winchester City Cemetery in the Gaunt-Taggert family plot. Lafayette Pearson was buried yesterday in the Pearson family cemetery in Lost Cove near Sherwood.

Lafe

Lafayette Washington Pearson
1860 - 1878

Lafe

Once't, when I wus born, I wus two people, Angel an Lafe together, all at tha same time, an somehow or other Angel weren't right, she could nair walk, nair talk, nair care fer herself, but I loved her dearly anyways since she wus me; so I went up in tha barn loft an prayed ta God ta make her right, an I cuts my arms an bled all over ta shed blood fer her, an I ask im that made us ta make us over agin, but He didn't do nuthin, we jus stayed like we wus; so's I became jes Lafe by myself, an I stays away in tha woods from Angel an Nanny an tha other'ns, much as I could; but all that happened a long while later, a long while after tha giant came on me on his big black horse outta tha trees; an when I think on hit, I still hyair his voice an smell im an see im killin my dog, Queenie, an then killin Daddy an Brother.

Nanny

Fer a long bit hit wair a mystery ta me, why neither of tha twins wair made right; they'uns jes weren't natural, they wair not hardly like human beins from tha first when they'uns come outa me, cept maybe Lafe he'uns seemed normal until what happened ta im, but you'uns could see Angel weren't. I studied on hit fer a long while an then I prayed on hit fer a long while an then, one day, hit come ta me, that hit wair a punishment brought down on me fer my ways with tha Garner boys, a long way back when I wus only a youngun an had nairy a bit of sense. But I guess from tha Lord's way uv lookin at hit I wus sinnin an had ta pay tha price. But hit don't seem right that Angel an Lafe had ta suffer fer my sins; tha Lord should uv jes done sumpin ta me an be done with hit but, no, them pore thangs, specially Lafe, lived most in misery; but thair's somethin good an different inside Angel that sumtimes I think's maybe like a real angel. I seed hit, fer she'uns wus always happy, even tho she can't tell hit ta us in words. Oh dair God, fergive me fer bringin tha sufferin on her.

Jeremiah

The first time I saw him he was coming straight toward me down a long field through the first soft-gray light of ev'nin. He looked like a young Viking: slender and fair with long blonde hair spread across his shoulders, his face as pretty as a girl's with full lips and long eyelashes; his movements smooth as water; his eyes pale, unblinking, cold and hard, the eyes of a killer. He wore patched dove-gray pants, no shirt and an unbuttoned, threadbare blue cavalry jacket and no shoes. In the crook of his right arm was a double-barrel shotgun, stuck in his pants was a Colt pistol and a long skinning knife was sheathed in a scabbard attached to a wide leather belt around his waist. He had two large brindle hounds with him, one on each side. He was fourteen.

Lafe

I wus four, when hit all happened. I still see hit an hyair hit...Queenie smelt em first; she set ta barkin, an runnin back an forth right side me in tha wagon, an when she seed all em horsemen a comin outa tha woods, she went ta growlin. They'uns so quiet at first, Daddy an Brother didn't see or hyair em, fer they're choppin on tha farwood but then tha horsemen rode up all round us an they stopped choppin. One of em was a giant. He wus on a big black horse an he come right up side tha wagon, right next ta me an I commenced ta shiverin. He look so much like a big bear ridin on a horse; I could barely see his eyes when they'uns looked down at me through all that hair an beard coverin his face over. He skeered me so I pretended ta be daid an hoped he'd think so too, an go away. But he nairy went. He reached down an grabbed a hold uv me an hitched me up an spread-legged me round his neck so's I's facin toward Daddy an Brother. All tha other horsemen had gotten down off their horses an were standin all round em; an when I see'd my Daddy I didn't call ta im or cry cause I wus daid.

Nairy a one hep me, not even God. Maybe He wus daid too, fer thair come a time way later on, when I knowed He'd died too. Tha giant's hair stank an, got grease on me an, I wus hurtin twixt my legs where I'd been pull't down hard. Two men, jes alikes, were beatin on Daddy an Brother while tha other'uns held em; then they started a cutting on em an Daddy was cussin an Brother nastied hisself. Queenie jumped from tha wagon through tha air an grabbed hold of tha giant's arm an bit im an he took hold of her an twisted her head an pitched her ta tha ground, an she nair moved agin. An I member tha mule's eyes gettin all big but thair bodies nair moved or made a sound, they'uns pretendin they'uns daid too. Then tha giant, he lifted me round in front of im an kiss me full on tha mouth an set me easy back in tha wagon an shouted at tha look alikes ta get thair hair an finish hit all up. Though my eyes be daid they seen Daddy an Brother's skin an hair cut off thair heads an tha jest alikes tied tha hair ta tha reins uv tha giant's horse an they'uns put ropes round Daddy an Brother's necks an haul'd em way high up in a tree, then they'uns all rode off. But I jes stayed daid fer apiece til Nanny an tha girls come. An when they seed hit all thair eyes got scairt lookin at what wair up in tha tree but I weren't scairt cause I wus daid an I hain't aire been scairt agin.

Lillie Jane

Lafe was killed when I had just turned four so I barely remember him. What little I do remember is mostly sad and unpleasant; the fact be known, he sometimes scared me. At night, when my sisters and I were in bed, we could hear him up in the loft talking to himself and making sounds that were more like a wild animal than a human. One time, I heard him in the kitchen with Angel–they were alone–he was talking to her like they were having a conversation; he'd make moaning sounds just like she did, as though she was talking back to him. It made me run and hide. He was different than anyone I had ever known, different, more than even Angel. There were two things that "marked him", as Nanny used to say about terrible happenings and what they could do to children: the first, must have been a horror, for he was only four when he saw Daddy and Brother being killed right in front of him; then they were scalped; my Lord, that's beyond my imagining. The second was Angel's deformity; Nanny told me how he tried to get God to make her right. He cut his arms until they were covered in blood. When Angel was not changed into a perfect girl, Lafe turned his back on God and even on us; he began staying to himself, sleeping for days out in the woods, hunting and killing animals, coming to the house for only a day or so and then he was gone again.

Jeremiah

Lafe has never left me. After all these years, there are times I conjure him up in my mind and see him standing in the doorway as clearly as I see my hand writing, his beautiful face, his pale eyes fixed on mine, his dogs by his side; I hear his voice demanding, '*Now, by God, tell me why yair hyair?'* For a moment I tense up, as I did long ago, then he is gone.

How could this strange boy have been my wife's brother? It was as if he and Lillie Jane came from different parents; he was fair, somber, easy to anger, with the language of the mountains; she was dark, smiling, filled with laughter and color whose speech is that of one who is well educated, which she is.

When I was with Lafe I was careful with my words and movements. He could be abrupt and would flare up if anyone, even his mother, opposed him. Yet with all of this, I was awed by his independence, his brilliance in the wild and his harsh honesty; the more we were together, the more I wanted to be like him.

When we were in the woods, if he sensed the presence of an animal or a human, he would throw up his arm for me to stop. Except for the flaring of his nostrils he would stand still as a stone; his whole being would be fixed on whatever he saw or heard or felt was nearby. His eyes darted back and forth; he sniffed the air like an animal; the tip of his tongue would flick out and twitch as he tasted the air. If it had been possible, his ears would have twisted and turned like a deer's.

Though I know it is foolish, it has gone through my mind that he wasn't quite human; yet I never thought he was insane or possessed. The old woman, Maw-ree, who lived in a cave on the side of the mountain, who some called a witch was with me when I first saw Lafe coming up the field. She said, '*Dat un comin der be a debil.*' No, that is not right; she was wrong, for though he was different than anyone I've ever known, Lafe was not a devil. Within him I could see the little boy, loving his father and brother who were slaughtered before his eyes; and I could see the brother whose heart was broken as he heard his sister, twisted in her crib, moaning over and over. How can such terror and sadness ever be known by anyone of us?

Nanny

After he seen Nathaniel an James kilt by John Gaunt an his trash, Lafe turned different an thair weren't a bit of joy left in im. An after he cut hisself all up fer Angel an hit nairy changed her, that's when tha demon got in im an from then on he acted like he ain't got no more carin fer anyone. He quit lookin at Angel, an if we'uns go ta tech im, he'd pull away. He even made a fist at me onct an had a look in his eye like he'd hit me if I laid a hand on im. He'd usually jest grunt or look away if ya said airy a thang to im. His eyes'd git all dead lookin an, at night, when he wus in tha loft, he'd laugh an holler an shout blackguards an thair's times he'd growl an his voice'd go deep inside im like he wus someone else.

All those last yairs, fore he wus kilt, he'd hardly hit a lick ta hep us with tha stock or crops. Tha biggest part uv his time wus spent with his dogs an guns back in tha woods an on tha mountin. When he'd kill somethin he bloodied his face an put tha meat on tha table an ud start actin out how he'd kilt hit an cut hit's throat; an he'd git ta makin tha gun sounds an tha dyin sounds. His eyes'd be all big an shiny til he stopped then they'd go daid agin an he'd go up ta tha loft, an fall asleep. Lookin back on hit all, hit aire a great sadness–fer he wair my baby boy...my baby boy.

Lafe

Tha Cove's full uv spirits, specially in tha cave or mongst tha beeches whair tha Injuns worshiped. Tha spirits nairy trouble me fer I leave em offerins on tha oak tree atop tha cliff above tha Sink.

Jeremiah

"Shit, yer still a kid an don't know nairy bout killin but by God I'll turn ya inta a killer. We'll kill that sumbitch Sheriff an tha otherns." That's what Lafe promised me. The next morning he took me into the woods above the Sink to a tree where he had hung carcasses, skulls, skins of animals and feathers of birds. While I watched, he circled the tree chanting over and over, " Tutsihusi, Tutsihusi, Tutsihusi," a Cherokee word that meant, "Die...die...die."

I killed my first deer, a doe, a week later. As we knelt beside her Lafe put both of his hands on her body, closed his eyes and said something that sounded like another language then pulled his knife from its scabbard, cut her throat and let the blood flow over his hands. He lifted them, turned to me and rubbed the blood over my face and in my hair. "Now, ye be baptized in tha name of tha one who loves killers." With that, he sliced her stomach open, reached inside, cut her heart out and handed it to me. "Eat hit! Eat ever speck uv hit!"

Three years later, when I was fourteen and he eighteen, we killed a giant she-bear, the last bear killed in Lost Cove. She killed two of our dogs and nearly killed Lafe. When he shot her, she charged and fell on him. I thought he was dead. Just as she was about to bite him I shot her in the eye and finished her. It was quiet for a minute then, I heard laughter and Lafe rolled from under her, covered in blood, "Jeremiah, yer ready, hits time fer us ta kill that sumbitch Sheriff an em other sumbitches!"

Lillie Jane

On December 22, 1878, my brother, Lafayette Washington Pearson, and Jeremiah Vann killed Sheriff John Gaunt, his sister Lucy Taggert and her sons, Sam and Hubert Taggert, on the road between Sewanee and Sherwood; Lafe was killed by John Gaunt. We buried him beside Daddy and Brother in the Pearson cemetery in Lost Cove the next day.

Nanny

Losin yair babies might nigh kills ya; hit nair leaves ya; tha hurtin's waitin thair ever mornin right side yair bed.

The Spirit

From 1817 to 1828, the John Bell family of Adams Station, Tennessee, was haunted by a spirit that eventually became known as the Bell Witch. There were nine Bell children. Among them, eleven-year-old Betsy was the one most tormented by the spirit. On a Sunday night, after a day of preaching, Reverend James Gunn was invited to have supper with the Bells. When they finished eating, Reverend Gunn began to read scriptures; as he did, the spirit spoke to Betsy who was standing beside an open window—watching, listening and thinking.

Minister

Deuteronomy, chapter eighteen, verses ten through fourteen: There shall not be found among you anyone that maketh his son or his daughter pass through the fire, or that useth divination, or an observer of times, or an enchanter, or a witch, or a charmer, or consulter with familiar spirits, or a wizard, or a necromancer. For all that do these things are an abomination unto the Lord: and because of these abominations the Lord thy God doth drive them out from before thee. Thou shalt be perfect with the Lord thy God. First Samuel, twenty-eight, verses seven through twenty-five: Then said Saul unto his servants, seek me a woman that hath a familiar spirit....

Spirit

O dear sweet, sweet girl, hear if you have ears to hear Old Sugarmouth's dark words rambling on and on in the night, seeking to strip sins away with King James, driving Deuteronomy in and out of wood, plaster, air and flesh.

Betsy

Delicate and transparent as fine white skin are lace curtains finely woven. Delicate finely spun webs covering windows black with night. Delectably, deliciously delicate to touch, to taste, to wrap round face, arms, legs, to watch through, to rest a spider; delicate and soft as white, soft hands immersed in whiteness. Watching others gathered together to discharge their curse. Minister, father, mother, brothers, sisters playing their child's game, searching for that to stay that which pulls them together in blood, in secret in word of God.

Minister

And the woman said unto Saul, I saw gods ascending out of the earth...

Spirit

Heed my words one by one, if a god comes on the earth your young bush will be burned with fire. For often he will make you pass through the fire in innocence, binding your long legs with wild grape vines, his face above you sweating and grunting. O sweet girl, he who is continually coming up and out upon the earth shall be brought low before I go.

Betsy

Delectably watching him: tall, shrewd in his straight strength of body and mind. He listening intently without hearing the ineradicable rhythm of God's word, hearing beyond the tall windows open onto summer's hot darkness, beyond night winds' whisperings, rumpling lace and skin, beyond the peeps of beasts and men.

Minister

Then Saul fell straightway all along on the earth, and was sore afraid, because of the words of Samuel: and there was no strength in him for he had eaten no bread all the day, nor all the night. And the woman came unto Saul, and saw that he was sore troubled, and said unto him, Behold, thine handmaid hath obeyed thy voice, and I put my life in my hand and have harkened unto thy words which thou spakest unto me...

Betsy

Riding above the winds and sounds of night he sits: strong arms folded, left hand hidden, right hand white in the light of the lamp, resting gently upon his sleeve, gently upon an arm heavy with strength and pleasure. Neither fearing, nor hating, nor loving, listening only to the amazement of a remembering, reviving in whispers over and over.

Spirit

Blood of my blood, bone of my bone, flesh of my flesh, know you not you are the temple of God, if any man defiles the temple of God him shall God destroy.

Minister

Leviticus, twenty-six through twenty-seven: And the soul that turneth after such as have familiar spirits, and after wizards, to go a whoring after them, I will even set my face against that soul, and will cut him off from among his people. Sanctify yourselves therefore, and be ye holy: for I am the Lord your God....

Betsy

In their circle they sit as for protection. Bound not by hands, nor by the minister's paralytic droning, nor by the six sides of simple, though skillfully woven weatherboard that vertically and horizontally fixes their circle as a cross into the rich, red land; nor even by their common source of earth and blood, but by the known and unknown knowledge of their secrets. Larger than shadows he sits. Listening. A conqueror conquered in his own strength; he who conquered forest and land and family. Sitting. His face turned half away.

Minister

And if a man lie with a beast, he shall surely be put to death: and ye shall slay the beast. And if a woman approach unto any beast, and lie down thereto, thou shalt kill the woman, and the beast: they shall surely be put to death; their blood shall be upon them....

Spirit

You that have ears to hear, let them hear: the desolation of houses where the beasts of the forests lie and owls dwell and satyrs dance; hear the wild beasts of the air cry in their desolation and dragons in their pleasant palaces. Your time is near at hand. Your days shall not be prolonged.

Betsy

Shades of red and black and white flicker and fade. The lace draws tighter round. Dead still they sit. Watching. Mouths open. Wondering at the milk and honey under their tongues.

Spirit

O dear sweet girl: Hear rather the genesis and revelations that come flickering from my mouth; a serpent's tongue testing the dark for the hidden one who comes from the forest running, leaping, shedding his skin of sin, drunk in his tremendous whiteness; a new child of God freshly risen from the Red River, running, leaping like a rutting deer. My testing tongue tells he comes grunting in glory. He comes and goes in the dark. His shadow swirls and turns black.

Betsy

Will he not turn and see through the lace, a face faced by enemies smiling on suffering and winking their eyes, that hate? Yes! They open their mouths wide and say, our eyes have seen through the delicate and transparent lace and forest. Nothing has been hidden from those who watch in secret the bright red spot of light rising in darkness. Will he set his face forever away? Turn now and see through the tears and sweat that leave their drippings on cheek and breast. Sorrows and shouts have been heard and not forgotten. Let them not smile. Let them rather shout in joy for the joy given!

Spirit

The sounds of our beloved! He comes leaping over mountains, dancing upon hills. Flowers appear before him, singing birds are all around, the turtle's voice is heard in the land and our vines have tender grapes. He is a buck feeding upon lilies and I am the Lily of the Valley. The earth trembles and shakes.

Betsy

The breeze stops. The single coal oil lamp, clean and bright, mingles its scents with others secretly hanging in the still and heavy air and gives life to shadows joining together without definition or darkness.

Spirit

Behold! The hidden one comes leaping and dancing hand in hand with all things created in the beginning. He comes. He comes. Leaping and dancing upon the earth. The earth heaves and opens. Behold! He comes! He comes!

Betsy

Bound round and round with lace–squealing and panting for joy!

Minister

A man also or a woman that hath a familiar spirit, or that is a wizard, shall surely be put to death: they shall stone them with stones: their blood shall be upon them....

Betsy

To and fro, to and fro, to and fro, rocking in rhythm to the word of the Lord.

Spirit

O sweet, sweet love, dip now your hand into the Red River. Know you the hidden one comes for burial in water, love and blood. Know you his sacrifice is your salvation. Know you God's will. Rise and sacrifice an offering unto God, young, white, delicate as lace.

Betsy

Listening now to his eternal listening. With him, as one, listening to whisperings rending round all in all.

Listening to lace and skin tearing away layer by layer. Listening until at last all is stripped bare and the hidden one rises fresh and white—Listen!—Aha now they all listen and watch. And now all their mouths are open. Behold! Behold! Behold! He turns! He rises! He comes looking full upon a sweet, sweet, white face clean of lace.

Spirit

Hear now, you that have ears to hear! Hear now the leaping and the dancing! Hear now the genesis and the exodus! Hear now, the hidden one, coming and going in the dark!

Minister

Exodus twenty-two, verse eighteen: Thou shalt not suffer a witch to live.

Cracked

In a cracked mirror

We appear cracked and of course

Many of us are

Around The Courthouse

Old men
Sitting
Spitting
Old men
Sunning
Funning
Old men
Sassing
Gassing
Old men
Joking
Smoking
Old men
Piddling
Whittling
Old men
Lying
Dying

White Man's Burden Blues

O yaaaaaaaaaaaaaa baaaaaby, I got tha White Man's
Burden Blues,

I work like hell to give a fright,
I run around a lot at night,
I get no respect in the news,
Marchin's made holes in all my shoes.

I buy my sheets and pay my dues,
I wear a pair of worn-out shoes,
I got the KKK, White Man's Burden Blues.

A Klansman's life is full of shocks,
Folks hit on you with sticks and rocks,
My hands are burnt, my back's a loss,
Ruptured myself liftin' a cross.

Refrain

My wife's sulled up, she's always mad,
Treats me sumpin' turrible bad,
Won't wash my sheets, or shine my shoes,
Talks ugly 'bout the Wizard's dues.

Refrain

My kid is big on Civil Rights,
He dances ballet in flesh-toned tights,
Wears a ring in his left ear lobe,
And dresses in a sequined robe.

Refrain

I'm plumb wore down, I've been abused.
Hot Damn! The soles come off my shoes.
Unless, next year, the Klan improves,
They'll suck air, 'fore I'll pay my dues.

Refrain

It ain't fittin' to live this way.
If things don't change, then I just may
Go sell my sheets and take my dues,
An' buy myself some brand new shoes.

Refrain

O yaaaaaaaaaaaaaa baaaaaaaby I got tha blues.
I joined a new group, just this year,
They've rern't my brand new shoes, I fear.
They march a lot and charge a fee,
They're called, N. Double A. C. P.
I buy no sheets, but still pay dues,
I wear a pair of worn-out shoes,
I got tha WORN-OUT SHOES, PORE MAN'S BURDEN BLUES!
O YAAAAAAAAAAAA BAAAAAAABY, I GOT THAAA BLUES!

...some were really strange...

The Devil Is A Gentleman

The Devil is a gentleman on a fine blood horse,
He sits on an English saddle of course.
His coat is blood red, His weskit pure white,
His boots are knee high, His spurs shining bright.
Handsome He is with His coal black hair,
And close cut beard and smile so fair,
He doffs His top hat to all who He sees,
To rich and to poor for He believes,
One should not look wicked, One should look kind,
For His face tires easily looking wicked all of the time.
In the old days His face was so scary it made babies cry,
But now people smile up at Him, as He smiles from on high.
He knows He must change to keep up with Man
Who's changing faster than even God can.
Or so Man believes, he believes he knows all,
That God and the Devil are both falderal.
Now that he's lost faith in the hot fires of Hell,
Man just wants to text and to tweet and to send emails,
And talk on cell phones and spend more than he's got,
So now the Devil's a Banker, who lends money from a pot.
He leaves Hell every morning with gold coins in His purse,
And rides forth with a smile to see whom He can coerce,
With their souls as their collateral for all that He loans,
Which, one day He'll collect on and He'll smile at their groans.
For the Devil's a gentleman on a fine blood horse;
Who sits on an English saddle of course.
His smile draws Man to Him; His smile is so fair,
Handsome He is with his coal black hair.

CROWHUNTING

One last look from a dying crow's eye
reflects all within its spinning
fall from flock black and sky
blue through leaf green
and smoke white as
red red red red
flash fire
and fade
away

The Black Boar

Deep in darkness   deeper than shadow
          quiet
                    listening
Hearing dreams curve   relax
Then catch tight at last
On tusks   curving   always curving
          inward
                    tighter
Rooting time away   his small eyes burn
Remembering with fire
Almost the laurel thicket has light forever
          a burning bush
                    almost
But only blackness and dumbness
Grunting   slowly   grunting
Something that has no meaning

          over
                    and over
Wallowing deeper into the cool mountain
Of his birth   floating on dreams
His ancient reflection flowing away in darkness
          quiet
                    listening
Hearing horns blowing away the forest
          black
                    bristling

Eyes of a Hawk

Binocular

Monocular

Far

Near

They See

The Mouse

It Eats

DAMNIT

PART I

Though I never met Damnit, I feel like I know him. His mother is my first cousin Dale Spain. When we're together at family funerals, Dale likes to reminisce about his and Damnit's life together. Before going any further I think I need to explain that Damnit is a Turkey Buzzard extraordinaire. While he'd be listed in *The National Audubon Society Field Guide To The Southeastern States* as, TURKEY VULTURE, *Cathartes aura,* AMERICAN VULTURE FAMILY, here in Tennessee he's just a plain ol' buzzard. My cousin, Dale, is a human being.

Right at the beginning of their relationship Damnit had a bad falling out with Dale. I probably should have left that sentence out since it's sort of a poor joke that probably doesn't add anything to this story. Here's what happened. A long time back, Dale was a bird bander and on the day he and Damnit first met Dale had climbed sixty feet straight up a tree to a buzzards' nest to band some chicks. When he got there, and stuck his head over the side of the nest, one of the chicks apparently got scared and thought he could fly but, of course, he couldn't because he was covered in white down and didn't have one feather anywhere on him. Instead of soaring upward above the trees, he fell straight down for sixty feet where he hit the ground, bounced like a tennis ball a couple of times and, no worse for wear, jumped to his feet, looked up and began calling for his mama.

Well, if you've never heard the sound of a Turkey Buzzard chick calling its mama–trust me–it's probably the closest thing there is to how a demon sounds when it's all upset: a deep spooky sound like wind moaning in a cave or in a graveyard of a Lon Chaney movie. The reason they sound the way they do is because they don't have voice boxes. It's a rather horrible thought to imagine robins and mockingbirds not having voice boxes; we'd have ended up killing them off long ago if they sounded like buzzards.

When Dale finished banding the other chicks and climbed back down to the ground he was too worn out to go back up the tree again and put the chick back in its nest so he stuck it in his bag where it was dark–immediately the moaning stopped.

That's how it all started. And it didn't take but a few days for Damnit to begin imprinting on Dale. Like a child looking up into the eyes of its loving mother, so Damnit's gray-brown eyes looked up into the brown eyes of the one who would raise him from a baby, feeding him dead road kill several times a day, cleaning up after him, holding him, stroking him and talking to him–everything–just like a real Turkey Buzzard mother would have done. Damnit couldn't have ended up in better hands. His own mother wouldn't have cared for him any better, or loved him any more than Dale.

All of this happened when Dale was a young man, when he was about as fit as you can get. Now, he's old like me. In his heyday he was the premier bird bander of hawks and buzzards in Tennessee. Banding birds of prey–"raptors," as aficionados call them–was Dale's specialty, more like a priestly calling, more so even than what he did later on to make a living, which was being a Nashville policeman. He was known far and wide by bird watchers as the man to invite if you wanted a speaker who would bring out a large crowd at your annual bird club meeting. When Damnit began accompanying Dale, it was standing room only.

At this point, I'm going to digress for a moment and get a little technical before we move into how Damnit got his name and how he made his highly acclaimed contributions for the advancement of science.

Here's what the *Audubon Society Field Guide* says about Turkey Buzzards:

> L 28", WS 6', Adult all black; head small, naked, red, bill yellow, Imm. head naked, gray. Soars with wings held up at 2 degrees above horizontal; seldom flaps wings. Long, rounded tail and pale silver flight feathers can be seen from below. Finds carcasses by sight and smell. Gathers at nightly communal roosts in tall trees or towers. VOICE Grunts and hisses; usu. silent HABITAT Woods, fields. RANGE Resident in SE.

Audubon is Okay if you want something short and to the point but it doesn't begin to capture the spirit or poetry of buzzards like Charlotte Hilton Green does in her, *Birds of the South:*

> Sailing far overhead, on outstretched, immovable wings, then soaring in great spirals until lost to sight, it is a thing of grace and beauty. Seeing it thus, one longs for wings and the ability to glide through the blue with like ease and grace.
>
> Seen close by, the great ugly head and neck naked and red, the wicked beak tearing at a gruesome meal of putrid flesh, the buzzard is awkward, uncouth and

> repulsive. Much of its time is spent on the wing, so that we are likely to see the great bird sailing overhead hundreds of times to the rare occasions when we see it feeding at close range. This may be Nature's way of having the buzzard "put its best foot forward."
>
> The wonderful, soaring flight of vultures has long been a subject of study by inventors. The great birds are credited with being the inspiration of the American invented airplane.
>
> The wing of the vulture is an interesting example of a bird's adaptation. It is large, broad and rounded, as are the wings of eagles and large hawks and is adapted for soaring. At times the bird maintains itself in the air for hours without seeming to flap its wings. This aerial glide is accomplished merely by the bird's taking advantage of the upward current in the air and adjusting its wings accordingly."
>
> [Under the drawing of a Turkey Buzzard, she wrote,] "Turkey Buzzards act as nature's health officers in keeping the fields and byways of the South clean of decaying animal matter."

For what it's worth, my opinion is that Ms. Green knows her buzzards better than Audubon and that our Public Health officials ought to lobby Congress for a National Turkey Buzzards' Day.

Here's how Damnit got his name. Not unlike the way humans get their nicknames from little peculiarities in their behavior or some oddity of their face or body, he got his name because of a personal bad habit. Since it's likely that Damnit halfway saw himself as human, it seems fitting how my Uncle Buford came up with the name.

Buford was Dale's father and one of my father's younger brothers and a favorite of mine. He loved my aunt Sadie and their children; he loved dancing to New Orleans jazz, eating Beanie-Weenies and drinking Budweiser beer. When he died one of his daughters tucked a six-pack of Bud in his coffin in case he woke up. As a Dixieland Jazz Band played beside the open grave, his daughters came dancing from their cars swinging and twirling white and pink parasols all the way to the grave. Just listening and watching them made me proud to be a Spain.

But that was all to happen long years after Buford named the name that was to immortalize the buzzard. It happened like this.

It came about on a nice late spring evening while Buford was stretched out half asleep in a lounge chair, under a shade tree, sipping his third Bud. At that moment, like a wobbly heat-seeking missile, Dale's adolescent, no-named buzzard came hopping across the lawn under the powerful influence of his bad habit. He made a beeline for my uncle's feet, more specifically, for his shoes, even more specifically, for his shoelaces, for he had an awful fetish for shoelaces.

Eyes at half-mast, blissfully dreaming of his and Sadie's next trip to New Orleans, Buford was totally unaware of the approaching attack. Then, and without warning, came a terrible yanking and tugging at his feet; his left shoe was pulled halfway off; he felt a sharp blow through the leather; the air was filled with gruesome grunting-hissing sounds. It startled my uncle so badly he lost his grip on the beer can, dropping it to the ground. He jerked upright; with his eyes spread wide, he stared down on the buzzard's bald gray head and at the hooked beak that was violently tearing and pulling at his shoelaces–for a moment he was speechless. Then, with a sharp kick at the thing's head, Buford rose straight up in the air and gave forth a great shout, "GET AWAY, DAMNIT !"

It wasn't a pretty christening–it lacked holiness–but the name stuck.

PART II

As the months passed, Damnit grew from one ugly stage to another until he reached adulthood when he really turned ugly. But as we learn in life, beauty is not in the eye of the beholder; if it's there it's beneath the exterior; true beauty, as we like to say, is in the soul and character of the inner being. So it was with Damnit. He was full of love for his adoptive mother. As soon as Dale would come out of the house Damnit would begin making his most beautiful grunting sounds and would fly down from his favorite tree to walk behind Dale wherever he went. In the summer, if someone left the screen door open Damnit would stroll in and go from room to room grunting and hissing as he searched for Dale. Yes, it's true, Damnit was ugly as sin on the outside but he had a good heart and was beautiful on the inside.

His time for glory was about to come. And he was going to be in pictures.

Among birders, Damnit's and Dale's names were synonymous; if one name was called so was the other; they were bound together, like Watson and Holmes,

Tom and Huck, Scout and Dill, Harvey and Elwood P. Dowd. Their reputation spread far and wide across Tennessee and, beyond, even among people who did not like birds, particularly.

It began with a phone call. It was a crisp fall evening. Just as Dale was sitting down for supper with his family, the phone rang. The voice on the other end was clipped and precise; a highly educated voice, one that sounded rather like British aristocracy.

Now, let me digress again for a moment to tell you a little about our people. Spain blood runs way back in the South, all the way to the Cherokee–Chief James Vann to be specific; Indian blood mixed with heavy doses of Scot, English, Welsh and Irish blood. My grandfather, Papa Spain, was Vann's great, great grandson. Papa was a tinsmith and made stills and whiskey and raised fine hounds and homing pigeons. He refused to pay state sales tax and went to his grave never paying a penny of it. The storeowners where he traded paid it for him because they wanted to keep his business and wanted to keep drinking his whiskey.

The Spains tended toward being independent, strong willed, intelligent, country-loving people who believed in family, laughter, hard work, good whiskey, good hunting dogs, good cooking, good music and God–the latter, not in excess. Education was a little further down on their list; like God, they didn't go overboard on lots of years in school. While our degrees have climbed the last couple of generations, thank the Lord higher education isn't watering down our blood so much that we've strayed from our legacy of loving living.

I told all of that about the Spains so you would know that most of us are like Dale, real intelligent, no matter how much or how little schooling we've had. So it was that as soon as that highly educated voice on the other end of the telephone line heard three sentences come out of Dale's mouth, he realized he was talking with someone who had as many IQs as he did.

The voice belonged to Dr. Peter C. Cappanarie, internationally imminent Ph.D. and full professor in Vanderbilt's School of Engineering Department. He said he had heard a lot about Dale and Damnit from a friend who was a member of the Tennessee Ornithological Society, and if it was convenient, he would like to come out and meet with them to discuss whether or not they would be interested in participating in a Vanderbilt aeronautical research project.

It wasn't a full month later that Dale and Dr. Cappanarie were standing side by side out at Cornelia Fort Airpark. Both were staring at the sky through binoculars, watching a tow plane as it released the towline from a two-seater white glider it was pulling; the glider turned to the right, made a circle back over the field and right as it passed above them, Dale saw his red-headed child pitched from the glider.

Immediately, Damnit's broad wings made three quick flaps then spread them outward to their full span of six feet; with the tips of the long wings slightly raised, he began to rise upward upon the warm air currents, spiraling higher and higher, soaring almost from sight, then tilting, turning downward, then up again; never flapping his wings as he glided gracefully back and forth above the field; and every time he passed over, Dale could see through the binoculars the bald head turn and look down at him.

All the while this aerial display was unfolding not far behind Damnit, the glider followed near enough for the cameraman to film every movement, every twitch of every black and white feather of the bird's large wings and each tilt of its brown-black body.

Remember Ms. Green's words, *The wonderful soaring flight of vultures has long been a subject of study by inventors; the great birds are credited with being the inspiration of the American invented airplane.* And here all of that was happening to Damnit; he was an inspiration, a contributor to the advancement of science. It was exhilarating, a time of adventure and accolades; the quality of his road kill meals significantly improved; he seemed happy and satisfied.

But good things don't last forever, and satisfaction can change when there are other opportunities. I wish I could tell you that these golden days went on and on and never ended. But I can't.

"So, what happened to Dale and Damnit?" you ask. As to Cousin Dale, he's doing fine for a man in his late seventies, a little slower, a lot grayer; like me he's thickened up some from too much fried chicken and country ham, too many buttermilk biscuits covered with milk gravy and too many slices of pecan pie and coconut cake. He probably couldn't climb six feet up a sixty-foot tree, but neither can I. All in all, though, he's well and still has a good healthy laugh.

"And Damnit, what about him?" Well, as you know, if you've lived anytime at all, love can sometimes take a different turn in life, some say it can even turn fickle. It's sort of hard telling this, but six months into his commitment to Vanderbilt and to high-level national research, Damnit's fetish for shoelaces and Dale unexpectedly and dramatically shifted.

The summer day it all came about seemed pretty much like any other; Damnit had finished with his spiraling and circling and was nonchalantly beginning to glide downward to the Airpark, followed by the glider, when, through the binoculars, Dale said he saw Damnit look straight up. High above him was a second buzzard—and Dale swears to this—and the buzzard was looking down at Damnit and twitching its tail.

I think, seeing those twitches was the moment that Damnit suddenly realized there's more to life than mothers and science and being in movies and even shoelaces. There's passion and lust and, on that day, for the first time, both of these took their burning grips on him. And now comes the part that is hard to bear—without one look back, without one last grunt or hiss, Damnit turned sharply upward, away from earth, away from Dale, rising rapidly upon the heat waves, till he was high up in the sky, right beside the other buzzard whose wings tilted toward him, almost touching him, as they spiraled higher and higher, side by side, growing smaller and smaller, until they disappeared into the blue.

Forever.

I had planned to end the story on that single word—*Forever*. It seemed to bring a nice finality to everything, or as the saying is nowadays, "It brings closure so everyone can move on." But that's not exactly what happened. I'm afraid what I said about Dale is only half true; all the heartbreak that came into him is left out. While he makes a courageous attempt to cover it over you can see the pain in his eyes every time he's on the other side of the coffin when we're carrying another Spain to the grave. His eyes have that thousand-mile stare that you see in photographs of men in combat at Iwo Jima and the Bulge. The other give-away is that he can't help bringing up Damnit when a bunch of the cousins get to talking together after a burial. We'll all be standing there laughing about some misdeed of the departed when, out of the blue, Dale will say, "Well, he's still not come back..." and he'll start looking longingly up at the sky as though she might be circling above us trying to see who had just died. By the time he looks back down, all the cousins have quietly left, stolen away.

It's my belief that too much denial is generally not good for you, and I hate to say it, but Dale is way down the road in that direction. Buzzards only live about twenty years and Damnit left him fifty years ago. So, it's pretty clear that he needs help. Since the last burial, I've talked it over with his wife and she agrees that an intervention is badly needed. Because of my career in mental health she asked me to do what I can to get him some professional help. And, if he refuses, she made me promise to do my best to get him another buzzard.

The Last Giant

This Fable is dedicated to
George Edward Brazil
(the real JoJo)

There once was a time
when giants and fantastic beasts
and strange two-legged beings
roamed the earth,
a time when myths and legends were created.
In some places, in fabulous form,
life from those ancient times
continued to exist after the great Ice Age.
Such a place was the land of Kituhwa -
the home of the last giant -
the greatest of all the giants.

So begins our story...

The giant is old and angry.

He was born when the ancient creatures were still alive,
before the last of the massive glaciers had melted away.

He has lived a long time,
too long after the deaths of his wife and children.

All of the other great giants have died.

He is the last of his kind.

He is alone.

There was a time when even compared to the great giants, his size and age were unequaled. Few humans had ever seen him or heard him speak and those who had were far, far away. They could not believe what their eyes had seen and ears had heard; and later, when they attempted to describe what they had seen and heard, they were uncertain, “Whatever that thing was, it was monstrous, it was nearly as big as a mountain, with hair and beard like a forest. It moved as fast as the wind and nearly scared us to death. The ground shook and it had a mighty roar like thunder, then it was gone.”

Though the Great Giant’s strength is still unequaled, age has slowly begun to weaken him. These days he moves more slowly. His bones ache when he wakes in the mornings. He can no longer see the soaring buzzards and hawks, or hear the singing of mockingbirds and wrens unless they are near. The new ways of the world confuse and frustrate him. Without his wife, children and friends, the world is empty and he has grown to hate it.

True to his father’s teachings he never shows pain; he scowls and gruffs to hide his sadness; he never smiles. His face is as hard as granite; his craggy nose rises in a high crest between slate-gray eyes; his mouth is a cleft chiseled in stone. Surrounding this hardness grows a wild black forest of long, greasy, tangled hair and beard streaked with white. He is terrifying to behold.

His home is a gigantic cave near the top of the highest mountain in the land. The cave winds far back into a maze of vast, richly paneled rooms filled with gracefully carved oak and walnut furniture. From the ceilings hang sparkling crystal stalactites that reflect the light of thousands of flaming candles standing in copper and iron chandeliers and candelabras.

From his mountaintop the Great Giant looks down on the forest-covered mountains that roll far away until they disappear into the smoky mist. Wilderness stretches as far as the eye can see, a land of waterfalls, rivers, lakes, fields and primeval forests of towering tulip poplars, chestnuts, maples, hemlocks, pines, oaks—trees that reach a hundred feet into the air, making a canopy above the forest floor that is strewn with ferns, mountain laurel, rhododendron, flaming azaleas and blue, red, pink, yellow and white wildflowers. Birds flit about and swoop everywhere; the air is filled with the calling of warblers, wrens, orioles, woodpeckers, thrushes and hawks. Insects and mice, salamanders, snakes, bear, panthers, wolves, elk, buffalo, deer, bobcats—big animals and small—roam the forest day and night, hiding from or seeking one another, building nests, lairs and dens; storing food; and playing and giving birth.

The Great Giant's world of Kituhwa is where once only giants and the little people and prehistoric creatures lived. He remembers the ancient beasts: the enormous, long-tusked mastodons and woolly mammoth; the fearsome saber-toothed tigers; the buffalo, elk, lions and wolves that were many times larger than those that live now; and, especially, he remembers the immense reptiles that shook the earth and the lumbering birds—some with teeth—that moved through the air. They were magnificent. But they are all gone now. They have died over the last millions of years, beginning when the earth changed and the sky turned black, the air, trees, grass and water were poisoned; then later, in the days of the immense glaciers, when the two-leggeds killed with sharp stones and bones and wood; and finally, when the greatest of the killers—the humans—came and spread across the earth with guns and fire and disease.

It was when the humans came that that which the giant could never have imagined happened. His wife and five children died from the black disease of the humans. She was the last to die. As he held her in his arms she asked him to forgive the humans and to promise he would not kill them. For a moment he did not speak, then he whispered, "I forgive them." But he did not mean it. This was a lie: "And I promise not to kill them." This was a promise to her that he would keep. Forever. She saw this in his eyes and reached up to touch his tears and died.

If not for his promise to his wife the giant would have slain them all. Instead, he withdrew to his cave. He and the little people, who hide deep in the earth, are the only ancient ones remaining. New life, in endless forms more beautiful and wonderful, was coming to replace the old. As he looks down on a world that has changed so greatly, his loneliness becomes unbearable and the sadness and anger within him at times bursts forth into a roar that carries beyond the farthest mountain.

He cannot bear the coming of night when his family sometimes appears and stands without speaking just beyond the edge of the light. He sees them standing there side by side, holding hands, smiling at him. And though he knows what will happen, he always rises from his rocker and walks toward them, holding out his hands, calling their names. Then just as he reaches out to touch them, they disappear. And when he calls, they are gone.

Though he knows they are only ghosts, they seem so real he cannot keep from crying. When they are gone he shuffles back to the rocker and slumps down in it and stares into the fire at the hypnotic flickering of the red and yellow flames, hoping that they and the long deep drinks he takes from the clay jug, will put him to sleep—and, eventually, they do.

On a late winter night as he dozes in his rocker, nodding in a fitful sleep, half awake, half asleep, he sees his wife's face in the flickering flames, her lips pursed to kiss him, then an ember pops and he jerks fully awake. He leans forward, peers into the flames and sees nothing, turns in his chair, looks into the shadows and listens but the only sound he hears is the popping of burning logs.

Oh, God, my soul dies. He lifts the jug for a long drink. His eyes close. His chin lowers to his chest. His breathing deepens. The flames die. Darkness and silence fill the room. He sleeps....

WHACK-WHACK-WHACK

Three loud knocks at the door. The giant sleeps on. The whacking comes again. This time louder, faster, nonstop. He lurches to his feet, turning the rocker over with a crash.

"JOVE'S BELLS, SHUT UP! I'M COMING, SO SHUT UP!"

He lights a lantern, picks up a large piece of firewood, stomps to the door and swings it open. Peering angrily into the dark, he sees nothing.

But just as he is about to slam the door, he is startled by a high-pitched, raspy squawking:

EXCUSE ME PLEASE, SIR, EXCUSE ME; PLEASE EXCUSE ME."

Startled by the horrible sound the giant quickly steps backward. *What in the devil was that?* It had come from just in front of his boots. Raising the firewood above his head, ready to strike, he steps back to the door and holds the lantern out and looks down. The light reveals one of God's ugliest creations–a turkey buzzard. Its small wrinkled red head and neck rises above a large body covered with brownish-black feathers. The buzzard is tilted slightly to its left to favor a sagging wing that was dragging the ground. It is hideous. The giant is speechless. *The Lord Almighty! Am I still asleep? Is this thing a nightmare?* He does not move or breathe. He stares at the creature, unable to believe his eyes.

"I say, EXCUSE ME, SIR! I know it's awful late and I'm probably disturbing your sleep, and for that I'm most apologetic, but you see I'm in a bit of a fix. Well, really it's a little more than that; I'm about to get eaten alive and sure could use some help. "EXCUSE ME, SIR! I don't believe we've ever been formally introduced. My name's JoJo, and I'm a turkey buzzard, which you've probably already figured out, and as I'm sure you've also deduced, something's bad wrong with my wing. It's a tad droopy, yes, it is; it sure is, and that's because it's broken, and that's because somehow or another I fell off a limb in the dark because...well, you get the picture. And have I said yet how thankful I'll be if you'd put me up for the night, for I am telling you here and now that sure as God made all creatures great and small and some of them are mean as snakes–no offense, sir, if your best friend is a snake. Anyhow, one of God's mean creatures is going to eat me alive, beak and all, if I stay out here tonight on the ground. I assure you I won't take up much space and I can tell you're an awfully smart giant and have already figured out that I'm an easy-going, quiet-type sort of fellow who won't put any burden on you if you'll just let me step inside and bed down in a tiny corner of your enormous abode. Yes, sir, yes, sir, uh-huh, yes. Sir...SIR...SIR...excuse me please, I don't mean to be rude, but...ARE YOU DEAF? AM I NOT TALKING LOUD ENOUGH FOR YOU TO HEAR ME ALL THE WAY UP THERE?"

My goodness he sure is big! In fact, he's the biggest giant I've ever seen...of course, now that I think about it, it's been an awfully long time since I've seen a giant. Man, he's big. Maybe my voice ain't carrying all the way up to his big ears. Well, as my sweet mama always said, 'nothing ventured, nothing gained....'

"MR. GIANT, EXCUSE ME BUT I NEED SOME HELP! WILL YOU PLEASE PUT ME UP FOR THE NIGHT? THE GOOD LORD WILL BLESS YOU FOR TAKIN' ONE OF HIS LOST SHEEP IN." *Surely he heard that.*

As JoJo rattled on, the giant was thinking, *My lord, this isn't a dream. I'm awake and this ugly thing, this loud-mouthed, jabbering turkey buzzard is real. Dear God, what are You doing to me now? Are You testing me again? Is this another ghost? Instead of sending an angel, have You sent a crazy turkey buzzard? If You have I don't much like Your sense of humor. I've had just about all the tests I can stand...well, blast it, blast it, blast it...if he's not a ghost he's right. If he stays outside on the ground with that broken wing something will make a meal of him before the sun comes up. Am I losing my mind? Well, God, I'm telling You right now, this is the very last one of Your tests I'm going to take. And You better not forget it!*

After a long moment, he begins to shake his head like he cannot believe what he is saying, "Well, blast it. Come in and let me shut the door before all the heat's gone. Drag your miserable hide into that far corner and go to sleep. And you better not make a sound that wakes me up. I'm going to turn the light out now. Don't you dare wake me! DID YOU HEAR WHAT I SAID?"

"Yes, sir; yes, sir!" said JoJo, as he lurched in dragging his wing on the floor. "Indeed, I do hear you; indeed, I do; and I'm grateful for your benevolence; and might I add, I'm beholden to you...yes, sir, the good Lord has brought me out of the wilderness and delivered me from my enemies to the doorway and protection of a good and kind giant. The Lord bless you for this deed, yes, sir, and might I add..."

"SHUT UP!" shouted the giant. "Shut up that squawking and lie down and go to sleep. And I'm telling you one more time: You'd better not wake me because if you do, "YOU'LL NEVER SQUAWK AGAIN!"

The next morning, as the giant begins to wake, he smells something–something delicious–he sniffs and sniffs again. *Bacon? Fresh bread? Coffee...what the devil?* Then he hears bacon sizzling, an iron skillet being moved on the stove, burning logs roaring in the fireplace. But above these sounds there is a high-pitched humming which grew louder and louder until suddenly it bursts into a screeching song.

"I may not be pretty,
I may not be sweet,
But ain't nobody can beat me,
At finding dead meat."

The giant raises up on his elbow and shakes his head. *Am I awake? Where am I? Oh my lord, have I died and gone to hell in my own house? Is that Satan singing?* But as his mind clears he has a flash of the creature he had allowed to come into his home during the night.

Exploding from bed with a tremendous roar, he shouts, "STOP THAT SCREECHING! WHAT IN THE DEVIL DO YOU THINK YOU'RE DOING?" He stops, looks at the buzzard, then at the stove, turns slowly and looks around the room and then leans over and looks down beside the bed—at JoJo. *That thing is grinning at me. What have I done letting it into my house?*

Smiling to the back of his head, JoJo hands a cup of coffee up to the giant. Fresh logs burn brightly in the fireplace. Bacon and eggs are cooking on the stove. The room is clean and neat. The giant is speechless.

JoJo points to the table. "Take a seat, Mr. Giant. Breakfast will be ready in a minute. Yes, sir, it sure will. And I dearly hope you'll excuse me for taking liberties, but in my humble way I feel a great obligation to repay you for taking me in and saving me from the beasts and demons of the night. I sure do! Now, if you'll just go over to the table and take a seat—the food's a-coming."

Dragging his broken wing, JoJo turns and totters back to the stove where he jumps up on a stool and begins to stir the eggs, all the while humming his little ditty.

Muttering to himself, the giant gets out of bed, pulls on his socks, pants and shirt over his long gray underwear and walks to the table, sits down and eats his breakfast without a word. Now and then, when the humming reaches the pitch of a raspy saw, he grinds his teeth and suffers in silence. All the while, out of the corner of his eyes he watches the buzzard washing and drying the skillet, a heavy bowl and a big wooden spoon, not stopping once to rest, and doing it all with only one wing. *That ugly thing's got grit. I'll give him that.* Though he knows the buzzard must be in pain, he does not see the slightest grimace nor does he hear one groan or complaint. JoJo just works and hums and smiles.

Remembering how his father had raised him to never show pain, the giant is impressed. He thinks, *I suppose I should at least fix his wing.* He continues to watch JoJo a little while longer then asks, "What did you say your name is?"

"It's JoJo. It sure is. It's JoJo. I don't know where my mama got that name, but that's it. Don't even have any kind of an initial. I'm just JoJo, just plain old JoJo."

"OK, OK, that's enough, I get it. Tell you what, JoJo, come over here and let me put you up on the table and I'll take a look at and try to fix your wing."

Thirty minutes later the giant finished setting the wing. Pulling it back into its socket, moving the wing back and forth to be sure it was set right, then binding it and putting it in a sling had to have hurt terribly; but the brave turkey buzzard never flinched or made a sound while he was being treated. When he is finished, the giant crosses his arms and with a firm voice says, "Look here now, I'm going to let you stay on until that wing heals, but the minute you are able to fly from the ground to a tree limb, you are out of here! No 'ifs', 'ands' or 'buts.' You got it?"

"Yes...but..." As the days and weeks go by, the giant gradually changes and is comforted by JoJo's kindness, laughter and hard work. At first he simply admires his toughness, then come brief moments when the buzzard's silliness makes him smile. But what touches him the most is JoJo's kindness. It seems it is in his very nature to be kind and it is this that begins to soften the giant's heart. And slowly, surely, the giant begins to realize that he wants to live.

Then on this warm sunny day, weeks after the wing has healed, he watches JoJo soaring high above him on the heat waves that are rising from the valley and he suddenly feels himself smiling and crying at the same time. As he wipes his tears and blows his nose, he knows he has come alive again and that he loves JoJo who has given him back his life.

That evening, as the two of them are looking at the sunset, the giant puts his hand on JoJo's shoulder and says, "JoJo, I want you to stay here with me and make this your home."

For the brevity of three breaths JoJo is silent, then he bursts into tears and laughter. He jumps up and runs, hopping and skipping, to the edge of the cliff and leaps into the air. Spreading his great wings he flaps them twice and rises upward, soaring higher and higher into the gray-blue sky and he begins to sing–and his singing can be heard across all the mountains and valleys of Kituwha.

In the months that follow, the giant is mostly happy; but there are times—and these times are always unexpected—when the formation of a cloud or the rustling of leaves or a soft breeze on his face brings a sudden sadness, a memory that draws him back into the past. Usually, these feelings and thoughts pass quickly and he goes on as though nothing has happened.

But one day it does not pass, and nothing that JoJo says or does turns away the feeling of loneliness that has come upon the giant. He sits on the stone ledge, leaning forward with his chin cupped in his hands, staring across the valley at the Beautiful Mountain. His face is filled with sadness.

Just as the last red and gold colors fade from the western horizon, JoJo flies down and perches on his knee and says, "What's the matter, Giant? Why are you looking so sad?"

The giant does not answer. He sits like a statue with his shoulders slumped, silent for so long that JoJo wonders if he is ill. They sit there as darkness comes and stars begin to appear. Still the giant does not speak. The air is turning cool when the giant finally sits up straight and says, "My beautiful Katrina died long ago...but right now it seems like it was today. I wish you could have seen how beautiful she was. I still miss her very much. There are times, like today, when I feel her presence...so strong. I see her face and hear her voice as though she were sitting here beside me—just as we used to—to watch the sun go down. As he talks his eyes fix on the Beautiful Mountain. He raises his right arm straight toward it and begins to move his hand back and forth in a stroking motion. *I still love you so much,* he whispers. He looks down at JoJo, “She is there you know. She is there waiting for me.”

It is all so real that JoJo looks hard at the mountain, trying to see what the giant sees; but he doesn’t see her. He rubs his eyes and looks again; still he doesn’t see her. “Giant, I can’t see her; where is she?"

“You are looking at her. She is the Beautiful Mountain. When she died I laid her there and covered her with earth and then I planted grass, flowers, ferns, flowering shrubs and young trees everywhere above her. And when I finished, I made a new valley beside her—where I will be buried.”

As he is speaking the giant rises to his immense height and sweeps his arm back and forth, pointing with his fingers toward all of the mountains that rolled on and on, like ocean waves toward the horizon. “JoJo, look at what I am showing you. Look at those great mountains that rise above the valleys for as far as you can see. They are my wife and children, my ancestors and friends. I buried many of them there in the Graveyard Of The Giants. Hear me now! When I die, I want you to bury me in the valley next to my wife. And I want you to lay me so that my hand is upon her. Will you promise to do this for me?”

For a minute JoJo was quiet; then, with his voice breaking, he said, “Yes, I promise.”

*****

The next morning, while the giant is still asleep, JoJo eases quietly out of his bed and makes a cup of coffee, then goes outside on the ledge and spreads his wings all the way out to catch the warmth of the morning sun. Over the valley, some teen-age buzzards are doing loop-de-loops and fast dives when all at once one of them becomes tangled in his own wings and begins to spiral downward, head over heels, toward the valley floor. JoJo holds his breath as he watches the terrifying fall; but just before he crashes, the young buzzard straightens out and glides to a safe landing.

JoJo lets out a long, "Woooweeee," and almost faints. He leans over with his head between his knees and takes seven deep breaths, then sits up and looks to see if the young buzzard is harmed.

A bright light is coming slowly out of the tree line at the foot of the Beautiful Mountain. As it moves out onto the broad open field the light glows brighter and brighter until it becomes luminous. One by one the young buzzards drop down from the sky and come to rest in the tops of trees from where they watch the light as it passes across the valley. JoJo holds a wing over his eyes to block the sun so he can see better; his eyes widen. He thinks, *I'm gonna faint; I'm gonna faint for sure this time.*

In the midst of the glowing light is a gigantic, white buffalo cow. She moves steadily forward through the long green grass. At the base of the giant's mountain, she stops for a moment, looks upward and then begins her ascent.

"Ooooh-oh-oh my," stammers JoJo, his eyes almost popping from his head. He jumps up and flies into the cave yelling all the way, "WAKE UP, GIANT...WAKE UP! YOU'RE NOT GOING TO BELIEVE IT... WAKE UP!" He lands on the giant's chin and begins slapping him with his wings. "GET UP, GET UP, YOU'VE GOT TO COME SEE THIS!" And he flies out of the cave hollering, "HURRY, HURRY, HURRY!"

Lumbering to his feet, the giant pulls on his boots and casually strides out of the cave. As he comes through the doorway, he stops dead still. Standing on the ledge in front of him is a magnificent being. Her whiteness shimmers as though the very sun is shining within her. Shielding his eyes from the brightness, he sees a spirit-being that is without blemish and glorious to behold. Her unblinking white eyes look straight into his. Then she speaks.

"Great Giant, I've come to you for help because you are strong and kind-hearted. There are many children in Kituhwa who need you. Hunters chase and kill their parents; children are taken as captives; some are trapped and sent to zoos; others wander alone, starving and with no place to live. I have found some of the little ones and fed them with my milk. Now I bring them to you, Great Giant, to take them and rear them as though they were your own."

While she is speaking, the heads of little animals begin to pop up out of her thick coat. When they see the giant they begin shouting, "IT'S GREAT GIANT...IT'S GREAT GIANT!" In an instant they are leaping to the ground. There are thirteen of them: two bear cubs, a black panther kitten, a fawn, a raccoon, two otters, a tiny red fox and five singing birds. As soon as they scramble to the ground, they begin to roll and squeal and chase one another around his boots, pulling at his pants legs, begging him to play with them. *"Please, please, please!"*

He is so befuddled he can't speak and does not move. He looks around for JoJo to rescue him; but, instead of coming to his aid, JoJo is jumping up and down, slapping his thighs with his wings and cackling so hard that snot runs out of his nose.

As all of this is happening, a strange feeling comes over the giant; a feeling that what is happening has happened once before, though he knows it has not. *What is it? There is something about the children. They are reminding me of something...something from long ago...when Katrina and I talked of having children. We laughed so hard thinking of all the silly things they would do. Oh, how happy we were when they came! That's it! I can hear her teasing me about how they would climb all over me and how funny I would look....just like they are doing right now.*

He stares at the white buffalo, then he looks at the children. He raises his eyes and looks across the valley at the Beautiful Mountain, then back at the buffalo. And he understands.

She is here. She has come back. It is Katrina's voice speaking to him:

My precious one, you need these children as much as they need you. You remember how we sat here in the evenings, watching the sunsets, and talked of having children and of the happiness they would give us. Your heart has been sad for too long; it is time for you to be happy again and to show your love and kindness. Take these little children and raise them. They bring my love to you. They will make you happy again.

Her voice is as clear as when she sat there beside him on those long ago evenings, with her head leaning on his shoulder. He feels her soft hair against his cheek and smells its clean fragrance. He nods, "Yes. Oh, yes! It is time for the sadness to end...I will raise them as we raised our children." He kneels down and cups his hands on the ground and the children run into them. He gently lifts them up in front of his face and says, "I want you to come live with me. I'll take good care of you. And I'll be your daddy."

He rises and turns to speak to Katrina. But she is gone. He walks to the rim of the ledge and looks down the side of the mountain; not seeing her, he searches the valley but she is gone. There is only the long green grass and the forest. He looks toward the Beautiful Mountain, his face wet with tears, and calls to her, "Katrina, you are my precious love."

*****

It is JoJo who introduces the idea that the children should live in the giant's magnificent beard. And, of course, it is JoJo who declares himself the supervisor of the children as they untangle, comb, clean and brush and brush the long, still slightly greasy, matted strands of his beard. They are exhausted when they finish and not a little tired of JoJo's incessant singing of work songs. But everyone is pleased with what they see: a big smile on the giant's face as he examines himself in the mirror. The beard is thick and soft and smells of honeysuckle and wild roses; it is a home and place that will become the children's haven.

The next morning, as soon as the giant finishes breakfast, JoJo and the children set to work on the beard; building nests for the birds; burrows and lairs for the animals; a large clear pool for swimming, with a twisting slide for the otters; hiding places; playing fields; thickets and woodlands; small hills and hollows. After a week of work, the beard is transformed into a home and sanctuary filled with laughter.

Near the giant's chin, JoJo oversees the building of a stage of his own design. When it is completed he takes his megaphone and announces that there will soon be a grand opening of "JOJO'S VERY OWN GLOBE THEATRE" where outstanding entertainment would be presented every Friday evening, including classical and original drama, musicals, ballet and tap dancing, magic tricks, comedy routines and juggling, all of which were interspersed with his widely admired impersonations of the humans.

While the children love it all, their favorite is on the fourth Friday when the giant tells stories about the old days, about what their ancestors looked like and how they lived. Sometimes there are heroic tales about the giants' battles with saber-toothed tigers, woolly mammoths, mastodons, bony-toothed birds with wingspans that could cover a giant's head, the great lions, cave bears and the fiercest predator of all, the massive-jawed tyrannosaurus. The scariest stories are of the two-leggeds, and after them, the coming of the first humans who could kill the largest animals with spears and clubs and fire.

One night, after he had finished telling a story, he sits silently for a bit, then says, "The humans are destroying the earth and air...but I believe a day will come when they will realize they must change or they will all die as the ancient ones died. If they fail to learn how to live together and if they continue to poison the earth, then...I wish that your beauty and splendid ways could help to change them."

* * * * *

That night, before he falls asleep, the giant's words keep going over and over in JoJo's head; he tosses and turns, and then it comes to him, *Well, maybe the giant's right and maybe he ain't. Sometimes the giant tends to talk too somberly. All that stuff about humans killing everybody was very sad. I could see it on the kids' faces. Talk about laying on a burden. I sure wouldn't like feeling that it's up to me to save the whole big old world. Lordy, that's grown-up stuff! But, then again, he may be right! No telling what those kids might do someday. Ha...watch out world, here they come. Ah, well, what does an ugly-as-sin turkey buzzard like me know about anything...well, now, hold up a minute, before you start putting yourself down, let's add it all up: you're the best class soarer in the world, you've got eyes better than an eagle, you're the best there is at cleaning up other folks' messes, you're the greatest stand-up comedian, pop singer, juggler and magician in Kituhwa, and when it comes to impersonations and ventriloquism and...and....* He drifted off to sleep.

The next morning, JoJo wakes up beaming with his first great thought of the day. It is another winner, so he says it out loud while preening his feathers, "What we need around here after all that awful stuff about monster lizards with teeth is a booster shot...what we need is a chorus with a world-class conductor and, as my ole daddy used to say, 'No brag, just fact,' that conductor will be me!" So, never putting off until tomorrow what should be done today, he sets to work on founding the world's first fully diverse animal chorus which he immediately names *"JoJo's First-In-The-World-Ever Children's Animal Chorus".*

Of course, there are a few things that need to be worked out, such as what kind of songs we are going to sing! Will they sing a cappella or will a symphony be needed to accompany them? Where can he get a tux to wear for their public performances? What size of baton will he need? There are so many questions he is making a list.

When he announces to the children that they are going to become world-famous as the first animal chorus, they go wild; they begin shouting, "WHAT'LL WE SING? WHAT'LL WE SING?"

When he finally quietens them down and announces that the first repertoire they would learn was JoJo's All-Time Best Buzzard Songs, they boo and hiss and laugh so hard at him that he finally shouts, "OK, OK, OK! Maybe they're a little too refined for you to start with, so we'll save them for when you have a little more experience. Since all of you are novices, let's start with some basic animal country songs. Do you smart alecks have any favorites?"

They invite the giant to their first practice session. After he is seated in his rocker, they immediately begin to sing without waiting for JoJo to raise the stick he was planning to use for a baton. They know exactly what they want to sing—and so, with each one singing in the voice of his kind, each one singing in a different pitch, each one singing louder and louder, each one singing beautifully. Finally, all of their voices blend together into a harmony of melodic wildness.

For a moment JoJo, standing on the conductor's perch, thinks he is going to fall off, or faint or both, he is so shocked by the harmony of their singing. Never has he heard such stirring grandness except from a powerful storm or the rapids of a white water river. He does not take a breath or make a sound. For a terrifying instant, he thinks he has had a stroke. But at the end of that instant his nature takes hold and he shouts, "HURRAH-HURRAH-HURRAH-ENCORE-ENCORE!"

The giant's chest fills with pride; his entire face is a smile.

When the children finish their third song, they motion to JoJo to come to them. They pull him into their midst and begin to whisper excitedly. In a moment he turns and walks over to the giant, "They want you to sing a song, Giant."

"YES-YES-PLEASE-PLEASE," they shout.

The giant continues to smile, then clears his throat and closes his eyes. And in his deep bass voice he begins to sing a hauntingly beautiful love song that echoes through the rooms and hallways of the cave. When he finishes everyone is silent. "That was my wife's favorite song...now, it's time to go to bed."

"We'll go. We'll go. But before we do, teach us the song and let us sing it one time with you."

He does, and they sing it with him and without another word, they all go straight to bed.

Later, as he is just about to fall asleep the giant says to the dark, "Tonight was special! I felt you here...you were right; they make me happy. Good night, my precious. I love you."

In the following years, more and more animals arrive at the giant's home for help and protection, sometimes singly, sometimes in families, sometimes in groups. Even the little people come, bringing their drums, fiddles, horns, songs and dances. From all across Kituhwa the weak and sick come, the old and homeless, the orphaned and lost. No one is ever turned away. The giant takes them all in.

JoJo and Mrs. JoJo, whom he had married three years after coming to the giant, and their fourteen children who are now grown bring their families and help build homes for the newcomers in the giant's beard and hair which has grown longer and longer and whiter and whiter until he now looks like a snow-topped mountain.

With the passing of time, the giant's body becomes weaker and weaker and his eyesight grows dim, but his spirit is stronger. There are times when JoJo and the others see a brightness in his face that remind them of the light that had come from the white buffalo cow.

In his last year they take complete care of him. He cannot stand without help; there are times he cannot feed himself. He is totally blind. During this last winter he is asleep more than he is awake. He eats little and rarely speaks.

On the first day of spring, he wakes from a long sleep and looks down on all of the animals and little people who are sitting everywhere on his beard and chest watching him. He smiles and in a voice so weak they can barely hear it, he says:

"The time is here. Today I must leave you. I have lived a long life and now it is time for me to join my Katrina, my children and my people. And you, my other dear children and friends, thank you for loving me and for taking care of me all these years. When I am gone I know you will continue to take care of one another as you have taken care of me and you will help anyone you see who is suffering or without a home. Never forget that we have all needed someone to help us. Be patient and kind and forgiving to everyone...I love you so much...now, help me stand and then guide me down into the valley. JoJo, where are you?"

"Right here on your heart, my good friend...my beloved Giant."

"JoJo, my dear old friend, you have been the lifeblood of my heart; your goodness brought me back to life. Watch over the little ones as you have watched over me...I love you...help me to my feet. It is time."

With all of their strength and gentleness, they lift him from the bed and out onto the ledge. There he stands for a long while, turning his head back and forth as though he were looking out over Kituhwa one last time. Then slowly, carefully, with the support of his "children" and friends he is led down the mountain into the valley. There they ease his great body down onto the soft grass and stretch his right arm out so that his hand rests upon the Beautiful Mountain. He closes his eyes. His breathing grows shallow and is slower.

And it is at that moment, that JoJo spreads his broad wings, lifts upward into the air, and begins to circle the giant's head singing the giant's love song. Then, in their tens of thousands, all of the birds rise from the forests and fields, joining JoJo in flight and song, soaring higher and higher into the clear blue sky, singing and singing until all of the land of Kituhwa is filled with song. All the animals and little people surround the giant, touching him with their paws, hooves and hands as they join the birds in the beautiful song of love.

The last words the giant hears are those of his children who stand on his shoulders saying, "We love you...we love you...we love...."

And there, next to his Katrina, and surrounded by those he loves and his wondrous land, the last giant dies.

But there is one final act of love to be done. So they begin. Everyone goes into the forest and fields and brings back the richest earth and gradually, steadily covers him. Then they bring seeds, grasses, bulbs, seedlings, shrubs and trees and plant them in the fresh earth.

And soon the rains and the warm sun come, and the mosses, ferns, grasses, flowers, shrubs and trees sprout and grow green and strong above the greatest of the mountains of Kituhwa.

* * * * *

It is Christmas Eve. Twenty years have passed since the death of the last giant–the protector of the animals and little people in the land of Kituhwa. His best friend, JoJo, now lives with his family in the giant's cave at the top of the highest mountain in Kituhwa.

For three days a hard blizzard has blown over Kituhwa. Finally, in the early night of the third day the wind ends–except for an occasional gust. The snow continues. Large, soft flakes float slowly down in the bitter-cold air, adding to the deep layer of snow that already covers the mountains and valleys. Everything is white. Everything but the tall black trees and cliffs and the great heaps of boulders that lie scattered at the base of the cliffs. Water is frozen hard as stone. Small herds of buffalo and elk cross the thick ice on the rivers and lakes. The herds make trails that are blue-gray briefly before they turn white again.

When the wind stops there is not a sound for a long while. Then, from far off, there is a sharp CRACK from the limb of a spacious old oak tree breaking under its weight of heavy snow.

A long wide valley winds southwestward through the mountains. The valley is almost free of trees and in the summer, it is green with grass and tall canebrakes that border both sides of the creek that runs through its middle. Herds of deer, elk and woodland buffalo come to graze here and give birth to their young. In the fall, when the grass and leaves turn gold, orange and red, the herds separate. Many cross the mountains to other valleys; but a few remain here in the forests that grow around the base of the mountains and upward on their slopes.

In the center of Kituhwa, one mountain towers above the others, a great mass that was once the home of the last giant. In the valley below stands an enormous black panther, staring up at the mountain. His eyes are large and yellow. They blink as flakes of snow fall upon them.

The panther is old but he is still powerful. His head is small and round with a grey mask and whiskers. The short black fur on his head and long back is white with snow. His breathing makes little clouds of mist in the air.

He is tired. He has come from far away in the west, crossing many broad plains, two wide rivers and many hills and mountains. Behind him, in the valley, his way is marked momentarily by his prints in the snow. Before him, through the falling snow and darkness, he can barely see the mountain. But in his mind he remembers it as it is in all of its summer glory. And he smells its greenness and the fragrance of flowers and the waters of many springs.

His long tail twitches.

The panther pushes forward through the snow, crosses the valley floor and enters the forest where he climbs a windfall and jumps down on the other side to the foot of the mountain. Here he stops, lowers his head until his nose is almost touching the snow and sniffs three times. Though it cannot be seen because of the snow, the trail upward begins here. He raises his head and starts the long ascent, moving at a steady pace up the steep zigzag trail. Halfway up he passes under a broad overhang. Here the scents are strong. He moves faster. He is almost there. He begins running as hard as he can up the final slope, then he leaps—his long body stretching out into the air—and lands on a broad ledge where the snow is packed hard and covered with tracks.

He works his way back and forth on the ledge sniffing at every track, stopping now and then, testing the air. Once he shakes himself hard, riffling the snow from his fur. He walks slowly toward the back of the ledge and stops, sits back on his haunches and purrs deep in his throat. His eyes close, *I am here.* They open and see an immense Dutch door: the entrance to the giant's cave. Light shines from under the door, sparkling the snow, and through the door comes the shrill sound of a flute.

A whirl of wind swirls snow across the ledge into the dark. The panther stands, stretches and takes two strides to the door, looks down at the light, raises his head high, opens his mouth, baring his fearsome teeth and...

SCREAMMMSSSS a long, high scream; and when it ends he screams again!

Immediately, the sound of the flute stops. There is silence. For a long moment nothing moves but the falling snow.

Then, almost imperceptibly, the lower half of the Dutch door begins to open. And, as it does, the light of a thousand candles shines into the panther's eyes and upon his body and into the darkness beyond.

He stares into the light. His eyes narrow, the pupils contract, he cannot see for the brightness. The air fills with odors. In them he smells a smell he loves from long ago. His teeth bare. His mouth opens.

"JOJOOOOO!"

"CECIL!"

The old turkey buzzard squawks, standing unsteadily in the doorway with tears in his eyes, looking at one of "our children" as he called the thirteen children he helped the giant raise. Later, when they were teenagers and seemed to always be stampeding over him, he changed their name to "The Herd".

The two old friends have not seen each other since Cecil left after the burial of the giant twenty years before. They are old now; their feathers and fur are turning gray; their wings and legs do not carry them as high or as fast as they once did; but their faces and smiles are still those of their youth.

JoJo, the sometimes preposterous, always talking, always lovable buzzard has a heart filled with kindness and generosity towards others. He is dressed all in red like Santa Claus; a long red stocking hat with a rabbit's white tail on the end sits at an angle on his head. His shining black eyes and smiling beak can barely be seen for the white beard that covers his face. His tall black boots come all the way up to his bottom.

Cecil, the panther, cloaked in black magnificence is a creature of power and speed feared by many and respected by all. Yet as he stands in the doorway of the home of his childhood and youth and hears the voice of one who was like a second father, he realizes how much he has missed his people and this land.

As they hug and hug and slap each other's backs with their wings and paws, JoJo laughs, "Ho-Ho-Ho!"

Cecil purrs, "Gerrrate! Thank God, JoJo, you're still alive."

Now the tears pour from JoJo's eyes, wetting his cheeks and beard. His heart overflows with the joy he is feeling for a child he thought he would never see again—and he has had too many hot toddies since sunset. As the tears flow he turns to the room and shouts—

"HEY, EVERYBODY, LOOK, LOOK! IT'S CECIL, HE'S COME HOME!"

For an instant Cecil is startled by the burst of light and noise. His muscles tense, he doesn't move—and in that instant he smells "The Herd."

They are here.

In his mind's eye he sees them as they were on that blue-sky day riding together up the mountain to the giant's cave on the white buffalo's back. He hears their laughter as they watched the buzzards doing rollovers and dives high above them. He feels the giant's cupped hands lifting them up, hears his deep voice saying, *Yes, you can live with me. I will raise you as my children.*

And as he is having these thoughts his eyes adjust to the light and he recognizes The Herd across the room waving and calling to him. They are all old too. The children he had kept in his mind are bent and gray and slow and very old. He sees what time has done to his sisters and brothers and for a moment he is sad, then he is filled with love greater than ever. Just as he is about to start toward them, JoJo leans forward and kisses him on the cheek, "Merry Christmas, my dear, dear child and friend."

With that JoJo leaps up, lands on Cecil's back and sits. He feels like a boy again, strong and energetic, without a touch of rheumatism. He leans forward, his beak beside Cecil's ear, "Move on, Cecil, to the sideboard...on the right, just past the Christmas tree. First and foremost we need to wet our whistles, Cecil, then on to The Herd...punch bowl, here we come."

They enter the cave. Once the home of the giant, he had left it and the mountain to JoJo and his children. Over time, as the children began their own families, they moved out to live elsewhere on the mountain or in the valley. Now only JoJo's enormous family lives here. As we know, JoJo is not one of God's humbler works. He can't help himself. He has pretensions. So he named the cavernous entrance room "The Great Hall" and the mountain "The Castle." But no one else calls it that. Not even his family. To everyone the cave and the mountain will always be "The Giant's Home". This was where he had lived his long life and this was where many of them had come for his care and protection. So they pay no attention to JoJo's airs, nor does Mrs. JoJo or their children.

But everyone loves JoJo, even more so now that he is old and his life moves towards its end. The head that once was bright red has turned white, his face sags, his feathers have lost their sheen and some are gone, his feet and legs are knotty, the talons cracked. His eyes are watery but not old, they are still the quick, shining eyes of a boy, filled with wit and joy—the same eyes the giant looked into the night he took JoJo in and saved his life. And on that same night JoJo began to save the giant's spirit.

The entrance room is immense. The vaulted ceiling is so high it can barely be seen. The walls are covered with delicate crystals that glimmer like spun glass in the candlelight. Stalactites and chandeliers made from elk antlers hang from the ceilings, iron sconces from the walls. Candelabras are everywhere. Tiny wrens and sparrows dart through the air with flaming twigs in their beaks, lighting and relighting candles. Massive wooden chairs, chests, tables and sideboards line the walls. Strange beasts and ancient designs are carved in the walnut, oak, poplar and chestnut furniture. The surfaces have been rubbed in buzzard oil; they gleam in the light of the candles. Far back against the rear wall stands the bed of the Great Giant. It is colossal. At night all one hundred and thirty-eight members of JoJo's family nestle and slumber in the bed.

A one-hundred-foot-tall white pine stands in the middle of the room. It is covered with decorations: glittering animals of gold and silver, popcorn chains, white paper angels and snowflakes, red and white striped candy canes, green paper flowers and small lanterns with yellow candles. At the top is a large angel dressed in a white robe. Her golden wings are raised high as though she is about to fly away.

Squirrels and chipmunks run out on the branches straightening the crooked ornaments and checking the candles to make sure a fire does not start. Under the tree are hundreds upon many hundreds of presents wrapped in large leaves, woven grass and strips of cane.

Behind the tree, jutting out from the wall is a stone fireplace big enough for two buffalo to stand nose to nose. Above it hangs a painting of the giant, painted the year before he became blind, by the top six artists among the little people. It is a good likeness, the hair and beard are as they were–wild forests surrounding a face carved in a cliff of stone. The animal faces peek out from his beard. In the center two little black bears are sticking their tongues out. There is a hint of a smile at the corners of his mouth. His eyes are kind, but they are sad.

Hickory logs burn in the fireplace. Before it sets the giant's favorite chair, his rocker. Garlands of green cedar and red ribbon are wound around the arms and slats. The chair has been turned into a stage for "The Little People's Band". They are standing and sitting everywhere, playing Christmas music with their horns, harps, drums, tambourines, flutes and fiddles. The others are on the floor with their arms linked as they dance in a circle around the rocker.

Animals and birds, even some reptiles and insects, fill the room: on the floor, the walls, furniture and in the air. Wolves, buffalo, weasels, bobcats, red and gray foxes, deer, bear and elk talk and laugh about the "good old days"—tales of who was the fastest, who could hide the best. The hawks and eagles, doves, geese, quail, crows, great blue herons, the turkeys—who have dyed their beards red, green and white—and hummingbirds, robins, cranes, wrens and ducks have flocked together in small, intimate groups. Now and then they spread their wings, comparing primary feather designs. They argue about the best twigs and grass for nests and which star formations are the straightest way south. The mice and chipmunks, opossums, the groundhogs and squirrels are telling and retelling their favorite stories about the giant, how he had scared hunters away with his roar and chased the flesh-eaters out of Kituhwa.

It is a scene filled with life: the old tell tall tales and nod off to sleep, the children run and scream, the young dance and join in singing with "The Beautiful Buzzards' Chorus"—or "The BBC" as JoJo has nicknamed them. He started The BBC after The Children's Chorus disbanded when they began to have families of their own. Under the direction of JoJo's oldest son, Bobby JoJo, The BBC tours Kituhwa twice a year and occasionally flies to performances as far away as New Orleans.

They stand in three lines now on the fifty-foot poplar log mantel above the fireplace, forty red-headed buzzards with ivy wrapped around their necks, all JoJo's progeny. They are just about to begin their next song. Their eyes are fixed on Bobby. His wings are raised for the downbeat. His fine tenor voice sets the pitch, "Mmmmmm...faaaaa...laaaaa...one-two-three-NOW!"

His wing drops—

"Deck the halls with boughs of holly,
fa la la la la la la la la.
'Tis the season to be jolly,
fa la la la la la la la la.
See the blazing Yule before us,
fa la la la la la la la la."

Their voices grow louder and louder and as they do, the singers raise their heads and wings upward. The stones reverberate every note; music and singing echo all around.

"Sing we now all together,
fa la la la la la la la la.
Heedless of wind and weather,
fa la la la la la la la la."

Cecil and JoJo stop beside the tree and look up at the singers. JoJo sighs and leans over to announce in Cecil's ear, "I swear, Cecil, that's the finest singin' you'll ever hear and ain't they the prettiest buzzards you've ever seen. I'm tellin' you, my ol' Daddy had it right, like he did about most things, when he said to me, 'JoJo, blood tells!' and up there on that mantel is proof that Daddy spoke God's truth, they're my blood and flesh—I mean, just look up there, just open your eyes and ears. And, ol' buddy, they're all mine! If I do say so myself—and I do! That harmony and pitch is the best your ol' round ears will hear anywhere. Nature and nurture, Cecil, nature and nurture; they got it both. Like my ol' daddy said, 'That ain't brag, it's just fact!' Well, let's don't just stand here gawkin'! Let's get us a toddy before my tongue cracks off and falls out of my mouth..." He pauses, gulps air and is about to start up again with words that are already formed in his mouth and ready to come out when–

Cecil bursts out laughing, "Lord have mercy, JoJo, you're some kind of wonderment. You ain't changed a bit. You're the same old humble buzzard you were twenty years ago. If you'll just hush up a minute I'll ride you over to that toddy."

Cecil pushes through the crowd past the Christmas tree and the harvest table. The giant had made the table from four dark-stained chestnut boards one hundred feet long. It is heaped with food: every vegetable and fruit grown in Kituhwa, and some that are not, but not one piece of meat is there. No one–not even the wolves–eats meat. They are all vegetarians, just as the giant taught them to be, just as he had taught them to live in peace with one another.

If tables groan, the harvest table is begging for mercy under the food that weighs down on it: platters of baked sweet potatoes, corn on the cob, deviled eggs, potato salad, steaming bowls of white beans, pintos, butterbeans and green beans, turnip greens, black-eyed peas, corn pudding, fried okra, yellow and acorn squash, mashed potatoes, cabbage, willow baskets filled with buttermilk biscuits, corn pones, golden-brown loaves of white bread, tureens of gravy and applesauce, crock jars of chowchow, pickles, honey, molasses, strawberry and blackberry jams, plates of cheese, butter, walnuts, apples, pecans and peaches.

At the far end of the table the desserts are displayed. This is where the little people and opossums always go first. The opossums are especially bad about eating all the meringue off the banana and rice puddings. There are cakes of every kind: coconut, pound, jam, angel food, devil's food, upside-down, chocolate and fruitcake; and there are pies upon pies: chess, pecan, fried peach, chocolate, mincemeat, pumpkin and blackberry and cherry cobbler; and there are urns of boiled custard and spiked eggnog, bowls of ambrosia, plates piled high with oatmeal cookies and little gingerbread men and women.

Beyond the tree and next to the wall is an old walnut sideboard covered in carvings of flowers and grapevines. It had belonged to the giant's mother and she had given it to him and her daughter-in-law when they married. This is where the drinks are: earthen jugs filled with sweet milk, buttermilk and cider; and crock jars with wine, beer, tea and coffee. In the middle of the drinks are two large copper kettles: one holds fruit punch, the other has five flaming candles under it–it contains JoJo's steaming hot punch that he makes every year from what he claims is an old family secret recipe.

"There it is, Cecil, there it is! Get me up close now so I can pour us some of that nectar of the gods. That's it...now just a tad closer...don't want to spill any, it's too precious to waste, stop right where you are...HALLELUJAH WE'RE HERE...I'll do the honors."

But he has had too much of the punch already. As he is talking, JoJo hops from Cecil's back onto the sideboard and just as he is about to grip the handle of a mug, there comes a loud hissing sound–

"HISSSSSSSS!"

He freezes, pulls his hand back. *Oh, Lord, deliver me, it's The Voice of She Who Knows Best.* He looks up.

Perched on a stone outcropping high above the sideboard is Mrs. JoJo. She is looking directly at him. Her eyes are daggers. Her beak is a sickle. Her face is an executioner's. She is dangerous. Her head shakes, "NO!"

JoJo's head and shoulders droop. All he can hear is his mind saying, *'Oh, Lord-Oh, Lord-Oh, Lord.'* But The Voice of She Who Knows Best cannot be denied. He grins up at her. Throws her a kiss and–

Leaps into the air!

He flaps his great wings twice, spreads them and begins to glide around the room in and out of the stalactites and chandeliers, then soars upward, higher and higher, until just as he is about to hit the ceiling he rolls over and comes back down in a smooth glide–his white beard and red stocking hat streaming behind him–hollering over and over as he passes above his family and friends:

"MERRY CHRISTMAS, EVERYONE...
MERRY CHRISTMAS!"

Every eye is upon him, just as "The Great Showman of Kituhwa" is hoping they are. His heart soars as they wave and shout back to him:

"MERRY CHRISTMAS, JOJO...
MERRY CHRISTMAS!"

He is so excited he cannot stop. He picks up speed and begins to circle the tree once, twice, three times, flying faster and faster until the air starts to ripple, shaking the needles and branches, making the ornaments tremor and sparkle like starlight. And as he flies he bursts into song:

"Joy to the world! The Lord is come;
Let earth receive her King..."

And everyone joins in:

"Let ev'ry heart prepare Him room,
and heav'n and nature sing,
and heav'n and nature sing,
and heav'n and heav'n and nature sing."

It has been a joyful Christmas, a day of happiness with family and friends, a day of good food and drink, of music and dancing and laughter. Everything has been eaten; the plates and bowls licked clean. Bellies are swollen, eyelids are drooping; all the stories have been told. The jugs and jars of milk and tea and coffee and wine are empty and, of course, the copper kettles of hot punch are dry as bones.

It is time to go home. The candles gutter out one by one. The sleepers are awakened and herded out the door. There are hugs and kisses and last shouts of, "MERRY CHRISTMAS!" And everyone is gone.

But The Herd remains. Their special time has come. The night is almost over. And now–as they have on every Christmas, it seems, for all their lives–they go out onto the ledge to watch the sun rise over the mountains.

The snow has stopped. The sky is clearing. Just above the rim of the eastern mountains the first light is silver and gold.

They stand near the edge of the ledge holding hands. In the dim light they look down upon the mountain that is the grave of the Great Giant and then, just beyond him, at the Beautiful Mountain and the ridge that joins them. As far as they can see stretches the towering Graveyard Of The Giants.

JoJo has removed his beard. His smile spreads his mouth nearly to the back of his head. He puts his wing around his wife's shoulders and pulls her to him. Then he clears his throat and begins to speak loudly so that those who are half deaf can hear him:

"My dear, old friends, we have loved one another for a long, long time. We have laughed and cried together; we have helped bear one another's burdens and..." his voice breaks. He stops, clears his throat again, and goes on: "You remember when we were young how the giant loved to have a party—especially, at Christmas. Ha! Talk about your good old days, those were the good 'uns. Remember the Christmas a candle tipped over onto his beard and it caught on fire and we poured the punch bowl on it and made such a terrible mess and all he did was slap his thigh and laugh and laugh so loud that none of us could hear very well for two days. And remember that hard winter when the snakes wanted to den in his beard and I swear he took 'em in and I double swear that winter I had to sleep next to two hundred rattlers 'til spring came. He thought it was hilarious and there I was balled up in a knot feeling their fangs and rattles every time I moved and here we are out in this cold and I'm sweating just telling it...what memories we have...here we are, just like we have been on this day all these many years, waiting for the sun to come up, just like we did that first Christmas when he was blind. You remember how sweet his voice was when he asked us to lead him out here so he could feel the first sunlight as it touched the mountains. Just like we are now, we stood here on both sides of him with all of us holding hands. Then he said that little short prayer."

For a moment JoJo says nothing, then he bows his head and says, "Let's pray it together." And together they pray:

"Dear God, bless us all and God bless everyone. Amen."

When they end, no one makes a sound. They listen. From the top of the Beautiful Mountain comes the deep wailing call of a wolf. Before it stops it is answered from the next mountain and then from another and another until the air is filled with the howling of the wolves of Kituhwa. And as they call to one another, JoJo begins to sing and the others, as it seems they have forever, sing with him:

"Silent night, holy night,
all is calm, all is bright,
round yon virgin mother and child,
holy Infant so tender and mild,
sleep in heavenly peace,
sleep in heavenly peace."

As the sun rises over the mountains, their singing and the howling of the wolves end, and for a little while, the peace that has come to this land will remain.

To The Dogs

At midnight

Every night

Right outside my head
There's some dumb dog doing
Thirty sets of three quick barks
That really say nothing worth hearing

Though

Maybe

He's just staying in shape to

Some night

Announce

That it's twelve o'clock
And all is well
Since the world is going

Going

Gone

To the dogs

...some were really real...

It's Thanksgiving 1969
Journal of George Edward Spain
The Great Revival of 1953

It's Thanksgiving 1969

For Jackie

It's Thanksgiving 1969

I'm sitting here

In our living room

Warm and well

Smoking my Oom Paul

Getting a little heady

Trying to write a poem
Worth reading
A hundred years from now

Or at least next week

Something moving
Pulls my attention
Outside to the woods

Through the twelve
Large windowpanes

I begin watching

Last summers leaves
Floating   falling
Brown and dry

They pile on top
Of others lying there
And start to disappear

It makes me a little sad
Knowing

But for the moment
I'm warm and well
And hear our children
Fussing and laughing

And your footsteps
In the bedroom above me

Journal of George Edward Spain*

Stonewood Farm

Williamson County Tennessee

*Previously published in
Williamson County Historical Journal, No. 44, 2013

Introduction

Shortly before Christmas 1962, Jackie and I and our first three children, Brad, Lynch and Trina, moved from Shy's Hill Road in Nashville to fifty-six acres in Williamson County on Still House Hollow Road, a one-lane, gravel and dirt road, named for the whiskey still once located near the head of the creek that curved beside the road. As the crow flies, it was four miles from Leipers Fork. Our land and the three hundred forty acres across the road had been the County Poor Farm. Most of the original buildings still remained there, along with a small lake. A gang of thieves had operated from the old Poor Farm a few years before we came there.

We moved from a metropolitan city to a rural, almost wilderness area filled with all kinds of wild animals and unusual people. Within a mile-radius of our house, which was surrounded by heavily wooded hills, hollows and fields, lived a bootlegger, a moonshiner, a shell-shocked veteran of WWI, a lady of ill fame, a black farmer who owned a rooster that laid eggs, a woman who shot her husband to death, a few mentally ill and retarded folks and a number of good, good people, some of whom became life-long friends with our family. No one was boring.

Forests stretched for miles in several directions. Some maps labeled the area The Barrens. The original Natchez Trace, a game trail that eventually became a one-lane dirt road for Chickasaws; Choctaws; French trappers; long hunters; and Andrew Jackson and his Tennesseans when they marched to New Orleans to whip the British, zigzags through the woods along Backbone Ridge less than a half mile from our two-story fieldstone, board and batten house that we designed. It sat against a hill deep in a forested hollow. A few hundred yards along the Trace was a concrete block building called The Fire Tower Game Club. A hundred yards beyond it was a fire tower that was manned only during fire season. A nearby foot trail led down into the hollow where our local lady of ill fame resided with her father in a small, one-room log shack.

Some of our family thought we had lost our minds moving to such a remote place where our closest neighbor was one of the largest bootleggers in the county, and moving there with three little children. But this is what we had dreamed of and searched for—and finally found! The countryside was beautiful. Our place came to be called "Camelot" by our friends the Brazils. Over the years we added more and more animals: horses, ponies, a milk cow, chickens, dogs and dogs and dogs, a black goat that could leap onto a low roof extension of our house and then would walk on it, chickens, hawks, snakes, pigs, beef cows; we raised much of our food in a large garden and had our own milk, butter, beef, chicken, pork, strawberries, wild blackberries, wild game and, from time to time, rattlesnake.

None of this could have happened without Jackie who was filled with the spirit of adventure and, though she was an unpretentious, totally honest, petite beauty with elegance and charm and a soft southern voice, she could shoot a twelve-gauge Winchester pump well enough to outshoot most men. She could milk a cow and make butter; kill, clean and cook ducks, quail and doves; race a horse; raise chickens and a large garden; kill rattlesnakes with gun and hoe; make beautiful clothes and curtains and prepare fine dinners for our friends and family; and could have five big babies and keep them in line while teaching them to treat everyone with courtesy and kindness. She looked like Scarlet O'Hara on the outside and, when it was called for, could be as tough as Scarlet on the inside. Once you met her you never forgot her.

* * * * *

On February 20, 1963, two months after we moved there, I started keeping a journal in which I made thirty-three entries through September 9, 1986. At the time I began I was reading an abridgement of Thoreau's Journal and, in the very beginning, I aped some of his style and that of the English Romantics. It gags me to read the first paragraph. But, thank the good Lord, I quickly went to writing detailed observations and experiences of the people who lived around us, of wild and domestic animals, and of our family and it becomes more interesting.

The Journal is written in a columnar book that is bound in black simulated leather with a red spine and corners. It measures eight by ten and a half inches. The three hundred pages are lined in blue ink. Only the first twenty-six pages include journal notations, four separate pages have literary quotations and on page 298 are dates and descriptions of various snakes and who caught them. Though Jackie allowed snakes to be kept in cages in the house and would cook rattlesnakes she was not a lover of serpents. Once, when one escaped from its cage she wouldn't let anyone go to sleep until it was found. It was hiding under some clothing on the floor of the boys' closet. A number of the journal's pages are stained by red wine that I accidentally spilled. Was I sipping a tad too much? Except for a few added punctuation marks and words inserted in brackets, wording is copied exactly, including misspellings and incorrect punctuation. Blocked margins have been put in and, for quick reference, the dates are now in bold print.

I am now seventy-five. I am typing this early in 2012 for our children and grandchildren and a few friends who might be interested in reliving some of the events that are written here. At times, the wording is a little pretentious, almost sickening, but for the most part it's a decent effort. These entries are among my first attempts at writing and so I tended to imitate other writers I admired. My first poems which were written during these years were poor imitations of the great Welsh poet Dylan Thomas and the southerner, James Dickey. *To expand or clarify some entries, commentary has been interwoven into the text in an italics, sans serif font.* The commentaries may have some inaccuracies, or flat-out untruths, as I am calling on my memory of times long past. Also, Jackie would correct me from time to time when I stretched the truth in telling something and likely she was right; on the other hand, I believe facts can sometimes stand in the way of a good story.

George Edward Spain
Nashville, Tennessee, 2012

Family History

George Edward Spain

(October 5, 1936–)

Married June 22, 1956

Jacqulyn Katrine Burton Spain

(January 16, 1936–May 25, 2009)

Children

George Bradford Jan. 14, 1959

Thomas Lynch July 19, 1960

Elizabeth Katrine June 23, 1962

Adam Burton (May 30, 1966–May 6, 2010)

Matthew Darwin July 23, 1969

Feb. 20, 1963 Today, I begin with a task I have set for myself, hoping, not only that it will have meaning to me but also to those in later years that may chance to read these pages. This putting down on paper of experiences, events that strike my fancy and thoughts upon which I dwell has for sometime been a desire. While it is probable gaps of days or weeks will be frequent, this is of no great import, as such compulsiveness in my life rings false. Rather it is hoped that I may be truthful enough to myself, my family, and others to place here in the parts of myself and my life which influence my behavior. All men seem in some way to desire immortality whether in a life hereafter, their children, or through the monuments of their lives. I am not sure of the first, we pass quickly from the minds of our own seed (unless they can benefit from their remembrance) and the element of time eats away the faces and soul of all but a few. Could the writing of this journal be an attempt at grasping at that golden ring? *For the most part this is ostentatious claptrap, attempting to sound like Thoreau whom I've loved from then 'til now.*

Yesterday Judge J. Short told me a rather humorous though somewhat grotesque story about one of the former people that inhabited a hollow in our area. The man took ill and unable to recover from the malady was carried by his friends to the White Tower-Vanderbilt. Great was excitement, jubilation and turmoil created by his arrival. Shades of the Old Testament and Africa, the physicians thought they had a marvelous case of leprosy to poke at and exhibit. The bleakness of their countenances must have been disturbing to all that saw them the day it was discovered the man's friends (such an endearing term might not be best suited in this case) fearing their community would receive a black mark because of the several inches of top soil and general assortment of vermin, had washed their ailing comrade in gasoline before his presentation. The Judge didn't know whether the victim survived his petrol baptism, died of the malady or if they were able to get [him] dirty enough again that he might have a hope of living.

Feb 23, '63 The weather continues to maintain its heavy grip on us. With the exception of the blizzard of '51 I cannot remember a more severe one. It has been particularly difficult for Jackie and the boys having just moved into a new home in this rather remote area and to be kept imprisoned inside by the confounded confining cold. *I worked in the Department of Psychiatry at Vanderbilt and was gone most of the day.* It has rather severely tested the house particularly when it struck -15. We are anxiously awaiting Spring., our champion, to free us from this encompassing, uncompromising prison. Have the new pasture and multi flora plantings been struck death blows? Our complaints however should not even be permitted utterance when we daily see the hardship these poor souls around us suffer through. Yet, can it be that their having always lived within a closer margin, or rather a more simple existence, knowing little or nothing of what we now consider necessities, do not feel the pain which we imagine they are going through. But, if their energies are sapped by the demands of just maintaining physical existence how can anything be left for examining or questioning not only their lives but those of all men. It is probable that their endurance is in itself an answer. Hogwash. I'm getting sickening. *Parts of this are dripping with Thoreauitis.*

Today, heard another colloquialism from the Negro Dotson who owns the farm adjacent to ours. When asked if he would discuss my desire to purchase one of their fields with his father, he replied, "Well, I'll name it to him but I don't know..." I hope to get all such expressions down – for someday they will be buried along with their speakers.

Our life here we pray, will be what we desired when we escaped from the entangling net that was being drawn around us in Nashville. *This refers to a street full of Burtons who lived on all sides of our house on Shy's Hill Road. The lots had been given by Jackie's grandparents for those Burtons who wanted to build there. We built the first one, then more and more came.* Only time can tell if our decision was right or wrong.

The children are all so amazingly different. They give Jackie and me not only daily pleasure but the only real meaning, outside of our love for each other, to our lives. Job was a fool or a mean s o b for if God did to my family what he reportedly did to that poor man's I would certainly.....

I am convinced about my self centeredness but am working to uproot some of it. It's so ingrained that it becomes a hell of a job.

Feb 25, '63 Yesterday was magnificent. After such a beautiful day can Spring be far away. Mr.&Mrs. J. Dickinson, the owners of Montpier and four hundred acres and from whom we purchased our small farm had us to their commanding home to ride and to dinner.

They are a delightful family and are so relaxed and non pretentious that one quickly feels he is a friend of long standing. *"Mr. Joe" was one of the great characters of Williamson County. He loved life and loved to laugh. In WWII he was briefly captured by the Germans at the Battle of the Bulge but fell asleep in a snow bank and his captors walked off without him. Montpier was filled with fine, old family furniture but things didn't always work. I had to carry a bucket of water from the swimming pool when I used the upstairs bath. One night when we were there for supper the electricity went out and they lit the candles in the silver candelabras. We had just started to eat when a pet owl flew down just over the flames and up onto a high curtain rod where it perched for the rest of the meal. A giant bull moose head sat on the floor in an upstairs bedroom as a coat rack. Billie Frank, his wife was a social worker at Central State Psychiatric Hospital. She had a soft southern voice and was often surprised by her husband's unexpected actions. One Sunday when we were at the pool cars started driving up to the house. In a minute or two people and children poured down the lawn heading for the pool. Billie Frank looked quizzically at them, "Who are those people...o my...o my, they ah from tha church...what has Joe done?...o my, he's invited the whole church ova to swim." So was life with Mr. Joe.*

While riding [with] Jim Lesson [Leeson], a young man whom the Dickinsons seem to have taken under their wing much as an adopted son, recounted the beginning of this old home [Montpier]. Built around 1790 by a lawyer from Mississippi with finances thought to have been received as a reward in the part he played in capturing Aaron Burr. This is one of the few homes not restored to the point of decapitating the beauty of age. We were rather amazed to learn that they have heated the home during the foul weather, for the most part, with the eight wood fireplaces.

Our ride took us many miles over secluded logging trails which run through the surrounding hills. It is indeed a pity that my vocabulary or ability [are limited] to express the beauty that we saw. If only it could be preserved but even as a flower losses quickly its precious beauty and a young woman withers so I know the sands are running out for this my wonderful country. Part of our trail followed the original Natchez Trace Road. A hard gallop across broad straw colored fields returned us at daylights end to Montpier.

While the menu was not extensive in selection it was sumptuous in preparation and most filling. I must confess that during the hour or so prior to sitting down to the table I became rather light headed from too much wine on an empty stomach. Much hilarity was enjoyed among the men while playing billiards.

Jackie and I are both delighted with these kind people and hope to foster the development of a lasting friendship.

Jim Leeson was another "Williamson County Character". When we first met he was an intelligent, handsome, middle aged, former journalist, bachelor, curmudgeon. We became friends quickly, rode together and laughed a lot. I think he genuinely liked our family. But at times he could become so critical, so rude, that he was unbearable, most especially if his anger was verbally directed at you with his slight Mississippian drawl. While he had much good in him his temper would probably have led to his being killed in a duel in an earlier time. Our friendship was broken one day in November while rabbit hunting on Mr. Joe's farm with one of my friends, whom he had never met. He didn't have a gun which is probably good. As we were returning to our cars, suddenly and angrily, he accused me of always "using" him when I wanted something; in this case two of his beagle hounds to the pack that included two or three of mine. His cursing and anger embarrassed me and my friend. Finally, I said, "Shut Up!" But he kept on. I took my empty double-barrel shotgun by the barrels and held it up in the air and told him that if he said one more word that I was going to hit him. I meant it and he knew it and he shut up. After that we had no contact for a year until I called him to have lunch where we patched things up on the surface. But we never had him in our house again. He came to Jackie's Memorial Service - he was quite fond of her. In 2010 when he was eighty he shot himself to death near his house which was close to the Trace. His ashes were spread upon the Trace.

Feb. 28, '63 A weather prophet I am not. Following the last [Journal] notation we had our twentieth snow. Thank the Lord that there have been thaws in between. Spring, however, should be the more beautiful coming on the heels of this white wake.

Yesterday had lunch with friend Chas. Hailey and developed an interesting discussion on man's ability to make a choice. *Charles was a year ahead of me in Lipscomb College. He became an excellent teacher and an administrator in Metro Schools. A member of "The Herd", which was composed of six couples connected from our days together at Lipscomb and, as of 2014, we remain close.* I felt we confused ourselves in semantics though it was a lively topic which we will probably resume. My contention is that our choice is made for us almost before the opportunity presents itself and that the selection made is the only one that could have been made at that moment. Our genetic, instinctual, physical, emotional, educational and environmental limitations and needs all come together at that one instance so that only one choice can be made. He also brought in evolutionary progress being always toward something better. I will agree as long as our present rules and great expectations do not enter into this. Evolutionary change is continuous by the second and what is better is only that which is best suited for the environment of the second. Man, for instance, might be a complete flop as an organism 100,000 years from now. They say fowl can withstand greater radiation than many beasts (including man). Could be, if nuclear war ever occurred, the barnyard chicken might become superior unless man can artificialize his world which I do not believe is possible.

We are considering the purchase of a pretty little chestnut filly - American Saddlebred and an 8 yr. old gelding chestnut. A few days ago Mr. Bob Smith, who owns the filly, spoke very beautifully of animals and how they help man to love his fellow man better.

Bob Smith was a gentleman bachelor accountant who worked for Truman Ward, the owner of Maryland Farm where fine Saddlebreds were raised and shown, the greatest being the stallion American Ace, grandsire of the filly which I bought and named Lady. Bob had his very neat apartment in his barn located on Old Hickory near Granny White Pike. The night I drove Lady to our place in Mr. Joe's old truck a wheel almost came off and Jim Leeson who was following me in a car went and got a bridle and saddle and flashlight and I rode the recently broke filly home, almost ten miles away. I kept her until we sold our place sixteen years later. She was a perfect horse: gentle, beautiful, surefooted, comfortably gaited and had great stamina. Friends and family loved to ride her.

2-1-64 Today my grandmother, my mother's mother, died. She was eighty-nine and her face even in death showed her goodness. And so one generation departs to make room for the next and we all take another step toward our final destiny. I was the last to see her alive and knowing that she would be gone before the sun came up I smoothed her hair down gently. Through my mind ran words that she often remembered to me that I said in my childhood "That old bullfrog's going to get you grandmother." Once when a child while visiting her and granddaddy as was my habit in the summer I had shown this concern before falling to sleep. She had calmed my fears and tucked me in but never forgot. My mother told me the morning before grandmother lost consciousness that she had said "I'm going to leave today" and she did though she lingered for six days proving an amazing strength since she had no sustenance during that time. I loved her but to be truthful my grief was small as in so many ways she was already dead these last years. Her mind was childish and she lived in days of before. I know she was proud of me and because of this and her own example I must meet her great expectations.

Her name was Lillie Jane Turner Crossley. Her father, Jeremiah Turner, fought with the 7th Tennessee in Virginia with Jackson and Lee and was captured a week before Appomattox. She was a teacher. She married Levi Thomas Crossley, a Welsh seaman, who became a farmer near Schochoh, Kentucky. Their small farm is still owned by the family. There is a photo of "Granddaddy" with David Lipscomb and others on the front porch of Avalon Hall. He went to Lipscomb for three years and remained a scholar until he died. Brad, our son, has the bed he died in. He had a great influence on me, and the character Jeremiah Vann in "Lost Cove", my first published novel, is partially based on him.

2-2-64 We had no regrets, therefore, gr. mothers funeral was not particularly sad, in fact joy and happiness seemed to prevail. The life of my gr. parents and the care their children have honored them with is indeed a lesson. When contrasted with the torment of the Burtons what matters wealth, prestige and honor of the masses. Such things are hollow in the end. *Jackie's family was quite stable and loving but some of the others had considerable unhappiness.* I am proud of my parents for the love they feel for their parents and the honor they pay them. I am proud of my mother whose love for my father is indeed an example. *My father was very successful selling cars and was good to his family but he had problems as the result of drinking too much.* I am proud of my sisters for in them are my parents. I am proud of my heritage and pray God my children will be as proud of theirs.

Bro. Jim Bill McIntyre, a good man and a real Christian, a childhood friend of my mother, his father was my grandfathers friend, conducted funeral. Because of his personal affection for her it was the simplest and most beautiful funeral I have been to. I read two scriptures, one from the O.T. about the worth of a woman, the other at the graveside, the 23rd Psalm.

"Jim Bill" was the minister at West End Church of Christ for many years, a man noted for his phenomenal memory and loved by a host of people. He had some of my grandfather's religious books in his library. I visited and

talked with him less than twelve hours before he died at Lakeshore Home for the Aged. His memory was still good.

She was buried next to her husband. *(Whippoorwill Cemetery, Schochoh, Kentucky. My parents are buried there also.)* It was in the afternoon and we wore coats for it was cold. Lowing of cattle, the tinkling of their bells, meadowlarks, a Bible reading, prayer, we left and she was gone. Now half of that generation are gone, with only my father's parents living and they have become like smoke that will soon vanish. Then it is time for my parents. And after them -

May 5, '64 Lady bred to Mr. Joe Dickinson's Arab stallion Ali Bamus - Later lost her colt at birth Damn
The entry immediately below has no date and is written out of order but it is referring to the night of December 31, 1963, when the temperature dropped to near zero and seventeen inches of snow fell.

O that these words could read stimulate or open the door of feeling in the reader that I have felt. The frustrations anger, fear, relief, happiness would all leap forth. The Eve of the New Year was an event that surrounded itself, until its cup runneth over with a drunken excess of feeling. We went to the Fords in Nashville for a party, as is our custom. Snow began to fall in thick blankets as tho to warm the cold earth. In our enjoyment of friends we little realized that before the night was out the persecutions that befell Job would have only to willingly have been greeted with open arms. I must declare my behavior was very un Joblike. And so to the -

Great Trek – *For years our friends from Lipscomb had had the tradition of being together to welcome in the New Year. Around eight or nine pm a blizzard began and Jackie and I left for home in our Volkswagen Beetle, which was over twenty miles away. Johnnie Coffee, a live-in house servant, who grew to become our friend, was there with Brad, Lynch and Trina. The flakes were as big as cat's feet and coming down so heavy I could barely see to drive. There was no other traffic on Old Hillsboro Road. When we reached Forrest Home the snowdrifts covered the ditches, and I could barely tell where the road was. The wipers could not clear the snow away fast enough so we rolled the side windows down and reached around to the windshield to clean enough away for me to see. At that point we began to realize we were not only in deep snow but also in deep doo doo. The snow was now as high as the car's bumper. Another mile, and we came to the small hill at the Callicott's farm entrance and could not go any further. Mr. Callicott was an attorney who owned a large antebellum home and several hundred acres. I was just about to put Jackie on my back to walk the half mile to the Callicotts when a van loaded with high school students headed for their homes drove up and stopped and offered us a ride. The students and I pushed the van up the hill and we rode two miles further where we were dropped off with one of the boys who lived a half mile off Old Charlotte Road. I got Jackie up on my back again and with the boy guiding us we trudged across a field to his home where his parents, the Hydes, let us use their phone to call Johnnie to tell her we'd be home in the morning. We were given hot chocolate and a comfortable bed and the next morning we stood on the back of Mr. Hyde's tractor as he drove us four miles through the snow-covered land to our house and our children. We went through several snows in the sixties that were seven to ten inches deep; sometimes the electricity would go out and we kept fires burning in all four of the fireplaces. With all this, we had to feed our dogs, horses, cows and chickens and break the ice in the water troughs. On bitter cold, deep snow days we would bundle up and go sledding down the hill in the far field onto the frozen pond or saddle the horses and go riding. Few women could handle this kind of life and love it while raising five young children, but Jackie did.*

July 4, 1964 I believe this day that symbolizes our Nations Independence excited me as much as any that I can recall. The flags blazing colors in front of so many homes, the family gatherings and fireworks combined to make this a memorable day.

But in years to come this memory will, I am sure, fade into other July the 4th while the whiskey still that we came on when horseback riding will remain clear & undisturbed. Jim Leeson, the Armistead boys *(Bill and Bob Armistead)* had killed their first rabbits while hunting with us and the Old Natchez Trace Sissy Pack and I were riding in a deep hollow that ran parallel to the right of the Fire Tower road which is atop Backbone ridge. The still was located approximately 100 yards down from the presently unoccupied log cabin which until a few weeks ago was inhabited by our local lady of ill fame. Truthfully in her outward being she was as one of Macbeths witches with a gnarled, grayish father who would look perfectly at home perched on Notre Dame. The stream supplying the still is cool and surrounded by spongy mosses and fairy-like ferns that were many colors of green. 40 feet from [the] still, which is covered over from spying aircraft by the ancient forest, we could smell the sweetish odor of new brew. Sugar bags, emptied, littered the ground around the metal drums and wooden casks. The brewers, one of whom is running for constable, were no where to be seen tho this by no means meant we were not being closely observed. If they were away I'm sure our horses tracks will frighten them when they return. While this activity is by law illegal, among certain people - hill & mountain folk - it continues to be not only an honorable way to make a living but somewhat of an art. And who am I to throw stones, they are friendly people who do not bother me, and my father's father operated several stills and on one occasion was arrested in the process of constructing a copper pot for a still.

The local lady of ill fame referred to above may have been a Ms. Love, according to our son Lynch. One day, while Jackie was working in the garden, the lady came down the road followed by one of her customers who had a bottle in his coat pocket and clearly had been enjoying what was in it. Jackie said the lady was twirling a purple sash that was tied round her waist. She came over to the fence and put a foot up on it and began complimenting the vegetables, "Ummunh, those are mighty fine looking tomatoes!" and Jackie gave her a few and, "Ummunh, that squash is coming along mighty fine!" and Jackie gave her some. By this time her inebriated gentleman friend had come up and was looking over in the field at Prince, a solid black, beautiful, but hot-blooded saddle horse. He started asking questions about the horse and Jackie told him that he was high strung and had thrown me twice. With that, and with the confidence of too much booze, he offered his services to come and break Prince of his bad habits. With great pride he asked Jackie, "Do you know why I know I can break that horse?" She answered, "No, why?" After a slight dramatic pause he declared, "Cause I always wanted to be a cowboy!"

A few days after we rode up on the still there was an election day. The moonshiner who was running for Constable was shot to death the day of the election by his wife in their house on the ridge, just up the road from our place. She killed him for having an affair with her daughter by another man. It so happened that Jackie was again working in the garden when the Sheriff's car went flying by, headed up the hill. She continued working, but in a few minutes she heard it coming fast down the hill and as it passed she saw a man slumped in the back seat with his arm hanging out the window. A day or so later we heard what had happened and that the Sheriff was rushing the man to the hospital—but he was already dead. Not knowing their candidate had been slain, voters almost elected him Constable. He came in second. John J. Hooker, Sr. defended the woman on the grounds that she had done a public good as the deceased was such a terrible fellow. She served no time.

A quarter mile from the still is a large concrete block building where the Fire Tower Game Club meets every Saturday to follow that ancient but illegal sport - cock fighting. Our home is within one mile of these colorful activities and we regularly have contact with both the owners and customers.

Occasionally, after the fights, we would find dead roosters on the side of the road, but for the most part they would be taken away by a local black man who sold them as food at The Goat Cafe near his house. MUCH TO JACKIE'S OPPOSITION, I took Brad, Lynch and Trina to one of the fights, arguing that it would be "educational" and would bring history alive for them, especially when they read about Andrew Jackson and the cockfighting accounts in Pepy's London Journal. Thank the Lord it wasn't raided, as it was years later. Our friends George Brazil, Bobby Johnson and Joe McCllelan went with me on one occasion and can recall it vividly almost fifty years later. Inside the building were two fighting pits and tiered seats and a small concession stand. When the curved sharp-pointed spurs were put on the roosters' lower legs, the handlers would walk around the pit showing their fighters off and the shouting of bets would begin. This went on for several minutes then the cocks were placed on the ground about a yard apart, facing each other with their bright red or orange feathers spread aggressively out around their heads, ready to attack. For a moment they were held there, then the referee shouted, "Pit your birds!" and they were released and leaped into the air, flying at each other, slashing and cutting until one could no longer defend itself and a death blow was finally struck.

7-30-64

Folklore and Natural History of Williamson County (especially of the 6th District)

Our home is located amidst a wild tumult of heavily forested hills that extend like a chain from Nashville toward – The front faces toward Still House Creek which springs from a wooded hillside hollow within a quarter mile from the house. I have heard many delightful tales of the superb qualities of its water which at one time was the fount for a Federal Distillery. Numerous loose stones can still be seen scattered among the ferns and grasses which are the bones of the structure. Between the spring and our home (nearer the spring) stands an ancient but crumbling log house that reportedly was the main office and where [a] basement housed many a fine jug of legal mash. It is rather ironical that today, almost within spitting distance stands a smaller & well camofloged from ravenous planes illegal still. The cabin is occupied by two ancient & crumbling half brothers - The Thomases. One who is claimed to have once played the banjo on the Grand Ole Opry is steadily deteriorating into a somewhat childlike senile madness. He is a rather pitiful bearded old man whose enjoyments seem to consist of his gun whose reports periodically echo down the hollow and small animals that he loves dearly. Recently he had a baby groundhog which his younger brother whistled out of the den & caught. They subsist on his Veteran's check. In explanation of his behavior his brother once told me he was shell shocked in the war WWI. I could not guess. The younger Thomas is a knotty looking old fellow [who is] both pleasant & kind to young children. He loves to talk & as I pass by horseback riding he calls from his house & it is seldom I get away this side the half hour. Usually the Elder Thomas comes out & together they examine, explore, prod, push, lift & shrewdly calculate the merit of my horse, *a sixteen-hand, chestnut gelding named Natchez.* Following a thorough physical, prescriptions for his well being are usually forthcoming & I ride away wondering whether I should shoot the poor beast to get him out of his misery. They are great ones for wild game & both are to be frequently seen treading the road with their shotguns. At times I have seen them squatting Indian fashion back in a covered spot waiting patiently for some form of beastie. They also know the wild vegetables which they gather from the roadsides & fields throughout the summer. Is it necessary to say that they have enriched our lives & I hope my children will remember the two dirty but friendly old men. *I cannot remember what eventually happened to the Thomas brothers. I hope they were well cared for in a V.A. hospital or nursing home.*

8/1-2/64 Spent both days back in the hills on horseback searching for a downed plane. [Got] lost Saturday for 3 hrs. but finally found way to Mr. Joe Dickinson's. Lost Angel, *our female Great Dane,* about halfway along (Came home that night) but Satan, *our male Dane,* stuck the whole distance. Discovered hoof print of deer in mud of spring. Flushed 2 covey quail with many young birds half grown. On last covey one young caught in grass set up loud peeping & hen wheeled back in front of my horse (Prince) & went to fluttering in grass as tho injured. What a wonderful & beautiful sight, *watching her protect her young.* Undergrowth so thick after recent heavy rains could see little over 50' in some places. On the second [day] with large body of horsemen got pitched on my head when Lady tripped over obscured fence. Called in at 2:30 to announce plane wreck & passengers (Jim Reeves & ?) discovered near Franklin Rd. Both men dead. My rear has two large sores & hurts like blazes.

From this point on the reader will begin to notice the increased entries on wild game, most frequent are the sightings of deer. By 2012 the deer population in Tennessee exploded to the extent that they are now everywhere, occasionally even coming into Nashville. In the early sixties they were a rarity even in heavily forested areas. Turkeys were never seen, now they also are everywhere, along with coyotes, otter, armadillos and small herds of elk are being established in protected areas. For our family, who loved nature and wildlife, it was a great excitement for us to live in the country and to see wild animals. We saw all kinds of wildlife because we looked for them and learned how to see them: deer standing at dusk just within the edge of the woods, the white breasts of a Red Tail Hawk, perched far off, high in a tree, scanning a field for its prey, snakes coiled or slithering just ahead of your feet, bobcats, eagles, groundhogs, flying squirrels, red and gray foxes and the darting Coopers Hawks. They were all there and we saw them. Later we began rehabilitating injured birds of prey and obtained a Federal Rehabilitation Permit, taught ourselves falconry and, eventually, with a handful of falconers got the first falconry regulations established in Tennessee.

8/4 Deer from Cheatham Reserve are gradually moving into this area. Almost without exception everyone that lives in this area has seen one or more within the past yr. Yesterday Mr. Choat (?) said he saw 10 last March while riding at daybreak on Temple Rd. Latter part of summer '63 we saw beautiful large doe & her fawn cross road, late in evening, in front of our car. They strolled into a field & looked at us for several min. before bounding, flags raised, into the woods. Two months back the Owens *(John a stock broker, and his wife, Martha, were friends of ours. They lived two miles away.)* saw 6 in their oats. Several sightings on Old Charlotte by M. Bush *(lived near the Owens)* and Mr. Hyde. I have heard of 4 deer killed, three by men using fox hounds. This is bad, especially since they are just acclimating here, & I will report such goings on if I ever get proof. *A year or so later, while I was hunting rabbits, I shot three hounds chasing a doe. I did not kill them but peppered them good with my shotgun.*

Owens, our nearest close friends, spotted a large bobcat around 4:30 p.m. a few mon. back, running through the woods, cross a lane & go toward Mr. Hyde's. Seen clearly for almost a min. Guessed weight at 30-35 lbs. Bobtail, spots, gray. Others around have heard screams at night in years past. *Twice, when I was going to milk our cow at 4:30 am I heard one scream on the hill across the way. I'm not a scary person but their screams are almost human, almost like a woman.*

Elk & Black Panther - fifteen years ago, soon after nightfall, Mr. Bush declares he clearly observed, for longer than a minute a black panther within a half mile of his home on Old Charlotte Rd. A tenant also reported hearing the animal scream. *Far as I know Mr. Hyde wasn't a drinking man but I never heard of other sightings of a "black panther". Mr. Pearre, a fine man and good farmer with a high pitched voice, who lived a half mile from us, had years before we moved there, seen a large bull elk running in the woods. He had escaped from a zoo and eventually was shot.*

6/65 This past March at 7:30 AM four deer bounded across [the] road in front of my car. So intent upon them was I that I came near to running into a ditch. Their coats were gray which is their natural camouflage for winter changing to a fawn in summer which more nearly matches the dry summer grasses. They were all near the same size & as the bucks are antlerless at this time of yr. was unable to determine sex. They approached from the hill area behind John Owen's farm. I observed them grazing like so many tame cattle near the road that same afternoon. Got the children and took them back at 5:00 pm to see them. Individual sightings of these gentle animals continue. At present they remain in the depth of the forests due to the fawns. My constant fantasy scheme most of which never even get off the ground in reality has led to my toying with idea of establishing a small deer park here. At present too expensive but they would certainly be beautiful gliding among our trees.

Continue to consider possibility of experimenting with the new species of foreign game birds which appear to be suitable to this area. Past yr. Corresponded with our State Game Farm at Buffalo Springs. Three species that seem most suitable are Reeves Pheasant, an Iranian Black Pheasant & the Red Jungle fowl. I would erect a protective pen deep in the woods & hatch the birds under bantams & permit them to eventually fly away when they desire.

As a boy on Hillsboro Road where we had twenty acres, I had a large flock of chickens and sold their eggs. For three or four years I had a pen with a cock pheasant and five hens and sold their eggs. A few years after we moved to Still House Hollow Road, when we had a flock of chickens, I set some pheasant eggs under a Rhode Island Red hen but should have separated the chicks after they hatched out as they were so small they were killed one after another.

During the winter '64-'65 the whole County was in somewhat of a panic state over the high increase of rabid foxes. Several people & much livestock attacked by the mad ones. One man choked one to death with his hands when he was unable to escape. Within a mile of us 3 cows 1 mare died from rabies. In '63 across rd. Mr. N. King's *(Nathan King was Luther's more reserved brother.)* son [was] attacked by fox which he beat off with stick & killed with gun. During this period I always took a cane with me to barn & on walks but no sign. No telling how much money was spent trying to obliterate the population of foxes using poison, traps, fox calls & several dozen game wardens & 4 professional trappers. A few were sent to their reward & it helped the people to feel something was being done but in reality it was only the disease itself that would bring on the end. I believe that this is just another of natures methods to balance herself. Overpopulation leads to starvation & disease. Now for several mon. there have been no reports of attacks so apparently they have been greatly diminished. It appears that bats may be the reservoir for the disease & they transmit it to the foxes, skunks, etc. for there is a direct proportion to the number of caves in an area & the extent of rabid animals.

We worry more about poisonous snakes which abound in these unpopulated hills. Jackie killed one next to the house our first summer here. Not only is she pretty & sweet but quite brave for such a small feminine little thing. She struck at it with a hoe missed & it wiggled into a hole in [the] stone wall. Unhesitatingly she grabbed a hose up jammed it into the opening & opened it up full blast. It came out terribly angry but this time she didn't miss.

Last summer Mr. L. King, while clearing undergrowth 50' from the house killed a 3' rattler & then later a king snake [was] discovered 20' away constricting itself around a second rattler. It obligingly permitted me to move it & its victim into camera position for pictures. It then retreated from the battle field with the rattler which it ate. We now have a rule here: no black snake is ever to be slain.

Jan, '65 *This entry and the next one follow the above entry but are out of time sequence.* Mr. Burton *(Jackie's father)* carried Nelson, David *(Jackie's brother and his son)* and I to Kerrville, Texas for a deer hunt. The Y.O. Ranch encompasses 85,000 acres on which graze thousands of deer, sheep, goats, cattle & several species of exotic foreign antelope & deer which are now thriving there. In one day we killed eight deer. Nelson got three does, David 2 does & buck & I got 2 bucks. One small 8 pointer other large 10 pointer. At 4:30 PM spotted smaller bunch at 250 yards down from our raised position. He *(the 8 pointer)* was standing at edge of thick brush. Bowled him over with first shot & then out poured a herd of about 8 does who bounded on across opening. Then to our amazement out pranced a lordly buck *(the 10 pointer)* who nervously moved slowly across opening. He could not catch our scent & was confused by the thrashing buck on ground. I missed him 3x & then he stopped, looking back at fallen buck I nailed him. While intellectuals & others look on slaying of animals as rather barbaric I can only say that moment was one of the most exciting in my life. These being my first deer the guide smeared my forehead with blood. The larger deer reportedly was one of the largest killed there that yr. & in that season almost 2,000 were taken.

We had a thrill waiting [for us] that night because David wounded his buck & we returned with a pack of deer hounds to run him down. It was more like a picture of a medieval tapestry. We followed the dogs at least a mile before the large Airedale drug the buck down. When we got to them the confusion was fantastic. The buck reared, hooked with his horns, struck with his feet, snorted, men yelled, dogs growling & then he broke loose & charged right where Nelson and I were standing. He passed within 6' of me but the dogs were on him & in a minute pulled him down & a guide finished him off with a head shot. It was the end to a great hunt providing a tale I will probably tell & elaborate on into my old age. *As I sit typing this I can see the mounted 10 pointer's head on our living room wall.*

Now have 3 excellent beagles of which I am expecting great things next [rabbit] season. Rattler, my # one hound, has been bitten twice by rattlers, stepped on by a horse & run over resulting in a broken leg. He has survived all & he is now worth so much as result of medical bills I can't afford to let him die.

Nov. '63 Yucatan Hunt & President Kennedy's Assassination

Mrs. Burton, Jackie & I flew from New Orleans to Merida, Yuc. Where met Mr. Burton who had driven down with Mario, Mex. Guide who had been working for A.M.II *(Jackie's brother).* Due to hurricane from Gulf quail nesting washed out resulting in poor crop [of birds]. On previous hunts Mr. Burton killed as many as 40-50 a morn. A land of rock and thorn. Quite primitive land with numerous Indian ruins scattered among the sisal fields in which we hunted. Sisal is the main crop with most fields being hundred acres or more in size divided by loose stone walls. In moving from one field to another often the wall is simply knocked down & then rebuilt. The sisal plant is planted in long rows & has extremely sharp edges to its stiff leaves so that a cut to ones flesh can be most severe. The quail are smaller than our native bobwhite & when pointed by the dog they usually run so that to flush them the hunters must run leaping over rocks & plants to get them up. Jackie killed several *(She was Tennessee Women's State Skeet Champion for three years.)* but I was mostly along just for the run knocking down only two or three. One of our guides spoke no English but was a grade school teacher and quite kind and a gentleman. Immediately when we would stop to rest he would first attend to the dogs pour out water into the hollow of a rock & talking soothingly to them somewhat as they were well disciplined children. I got a start from almost stepping on a large snake called a ratternero (?) rat snake. Noticed that in almost every group of natives that were working in the fields there would be one man with a gun. They are always prepared for deer or wild turkey. Venison is included in all menus. On our way back to Merida from hunting one morn the guides stopped & purchased some meat being cooked in a large black cauldron which they shared with us. Rather like chittlings. Fresh meat hangs exposed in the markets where vultures sit on rooftops waiting for closing time when they swoop down in large numbers to clean up. The garbage men of Mexico.

I had intended to write something here in the Journal to tell how we learned about President Kennedy's assassination. I never got to it so—After a week of hunting, touring the Mayan ruins and going to a bullfight, we left in Mr. Burton's station wagon and headed for home, a drive that would take a week. We knew nothing about the President's death when we stopped late at night on the 22nd at a place that was pronounced almost like, "Thomas and Charley." The next morning, when I went down to get something from the car, an American made some reference to the President being shot. At first, I thought he was speaking of the Mexican President. When it sank in that it was President Kennedy I went upstairs and told the others. We ate quickly, loaded the car, crossed the border and raced for home.

1/8/66 fem. Bobcat trapped at Mr. Roberts on Old Hillsboro Rd. across from Callicotts. *(Mr. Roberts was a farmer who lived with his two sisters. He had had several sheep and goats killed before trapping the cat.)* Mr. R. accidentally caught the cat in a trap set to ensnare a hawk that had killed a hen. The hen with trap set on top were fixed on a tree limb 7'-8' above ground. During night the cat leaped from the ground to pull carcass down & was caught by the right foot &unable to get back down froze to death hanging in the air. She tore several claws off on the trunk trying to get loose. She was apparently in excellent condition as her coat was thick & long. Mr. R. gave the cat to the children & [it] was made into a nice rug *which one of our children has.*

Within the past year several bobcats have been seen within two miles of the house - usually at night time.

2/66 on way into work 7:30 AM 4 deer all hornless & approximately same size crossed road - one behind the other - immediately in front of my car so that I had to stop to keep from hitting them. They came from my left down old trail bordering Roberts farm & crossed over to the Callicotts. That afternoon they were grazing in C's front pasture & unconcernedly looked up at me. Went home got the children & brought them back to see them. Their winter coats were light gray.

11/66 on way to work with boys in car just past Callicotts farm looked over into front yard of old frame tenant house (part of Price farm) & spotted a huge (11-12 point) buck. Stopped & began backing as he gradually moved off down the yard holding his head very erect. He crossed road, easily leaped fence, flag up & bounded up stony hill toward hill area from which he had come. Boys & I were out of our minds.

1/67 Hunted on Moran farm (Moran Rd) with Mr. Kennie & one of his friends. *(Mr. Kennie owned a large farm bounded by the Harpeth River on two sides. When he ran for County Magistrate he brought his truck to where we voted in the small field at the corner of Old Hillsboro Road and Natchez Trace Road. He served fried chicken, bread and peaches free, out of the bed of the truck, and won the election, probably by a landslide. The Kennies attended Fourth Avenue Church of Christ where we went.)* Deer sign fairly thick - trails, trees injured from bucks horns (rutting season) hair on trees where they had rubbed. Almost froze. Had to leave at 10:00 AM to work and about 11:30 Mr. K. friend killed large 11 point buck that walked up on him apparently to feed in honeysuckle patch. A.M. & I hunted another day but saw no deer. Heard of 14 p. that has been observed several times on M. farm. Approx. 5 deer killed on that farm during 66-67 season.

Rabbit season fair but several farms nearly have been over hunted & supply sharply diminished compared to previous years. Hounds ran well.

April '67 Brad caught 5' rat snake & took him to school in homemade cage. During recess snake escaped into room which was discovered when class returned. Teacher vacated room with much excitement among children, especially girls. Brad and two buddies went in to catch snake & Brad grabed it by tail & snake whipped around & bit him, which nurse treated with tetnus shot. Snake finally caught & later sent to Mary Hill. *(Mary Hill Burton Dunlap is still living. She is Jackie's cousin and a herpetologist who was once head of the reptile exhibit at the Children's Museum.)*

Same month I had close call with copperhead. Pulling weeds on bank by garage after hard rain. Was about to pull group of weeds when saw a flicker - pulled hand away & saw copperh coiled to strike. He didn't. Apparently was somewhat sedated by heavy rain & coolness following it. Killed him with shovel, approx. 20" long.

May '67 Brad caught 4' king snake in back yard - gave it to Mary Hill.

Around 6:00 PM as returning home from work saw a large deer in our front field where he was grazing. Must have been a buck due to track size. I believe horns are shed at this time. He ran off through our wood & up hill.

Mr. Elam saw buck, doe & fawn early in morn that came down to drink from his lake. *(The Elams were wonderful people. They had bought the old Poor Farm's 360 acres across the road which previously had been owned by Vanderbilt with the plan to set up a Primate Research Center there. That not coming about, they sold it. Mr. Elam was the retired owner of Whiteway Laundry. They built a beautiful brick home that looked over a lake they put in below the old lake. This land has changed hands more than once since the Elams moved to Nashville.*

6/7/69 Got baby doe fawn from 2-3 weeks [old] from Luther King. *(Luther gave her to our children. He was Nathan King's brother and was a jolly man. He occasionally worked for us. He took a real liking to our family. He lived in Kingfield.)* A friend of his caught her on Lick Creek Rd. Dogs were chasing her. Health good. Frightened. Cries like a kid goat. Drinks from baby bottle. Named Bambi. Stall fixed in barn.

6 weeks later had to give "Bambi" up to State Game & Fish Com. As no permits given to keep deer. She has done well - no health prob. Eyes clear, very active - would play with children like a dog, running, leaping, watching them closely almost as tho she knew it was a game. Brad observed that her back feet almost right into the print of front feet when walking slowly. When she left was drinking 10 oz. 4x day. Also noticed she was on guard whenever any disturbance occurred, much more than domestic animal, loud noises such as thunder would cause her to stop drinking, go near barn window, sniff, body became tense. - sometimes skin would be shaking all over. Very friendly. Children were good about turning her over to game warden who was thoughtful & kind. Took her to State game farm at Cheatham Game Reserve where orphan fawns are raised.

Two does have been staying at the Elams. Recently drove to within 30 yards of them - they grazed for a minute, looked at us, flicked their tails & unexcitedly bounded away. Both appeared to be yearlings - possibly twins. Mr. E. has seen them by the lake several times, once one had a swim & later raced back & forth in a pattern "like a horse exercising."

Bobcats, by single & pairs continue to be seen, usually around Old Charlotte Rd. area.

At first of summer Brad & Lynch caught many non-pois. Snakes, sending several to Biol. Dept. at Lipscomb, however they tapered off with heat of summer. No pois. ones as yet.

At the end of the Journal is a list of snakes caught in 1969, who caught them and where they were caught. The list is in Jackie's handwriting. It will be placed at the end of this expanded Journal.

9/9/69 All back in school, thank goodness for Jackie. I continue to concern myself with some basic differences in my beliefs & those taught at Lipscomb i.e. the interpretation of man's blunders & faults resulting from sin (Lips.) or as W. Faulkner said, "man ain't got any morals, he just does what he's able." This later is not as pessimistic as it appears on hearing since man is capable of doing more - rising above himself - through the help of other men as is learned in all close relationships of love. Maybe the children will not come out so confused, rather if given the opportunity they can select the best of both sides to develop their own individual beliefs, for in truth the religiously convicted people tho sometimes doing little mean things have been & still are those most deeply concerned with helping others. Seldom does it seem that the man carrying the great banner & marching for the "general good of man" give the attention which is his responsibility, to those closest to him. Extremists are all alike - standing back to back, so close they cannot see they are touching rather than opposite extremes. Am reading The Man From Monticello & Men in Groups.

Last night when I was 1 hr. late arriving home, Lynch with his usual humerous ways commented, "Well, I guess he's out gambling again."

9/10/69 My first published poem Leningrad 1941-1942 comes out this month in Soviet Life mag. The editor of S.L. is presently first secretary to the Soviet Embassy in Wash. D.C.

It is interesting how motivation runs out for writing. I am very irratic going full blast for weeks then totally out of gas for months. As yet I have been unable to write something about Jackie & I do not understand why - possibly I just don't want to write something trite but rather make something with the depth (at least for me) of The Black Boar. *(The Black Boar is a poem I wrote. A local artist painted a boar and wrote the poem beside it and I gave it to her for Christmas.)*

Writing for me is very hard as I have done enough reading to realize my own poverty such as the first of this journ. Which smacks of 17th Cent. England. I must have started it on a romantic binge. Yet I know the real basis - I don't want to completely & totally die doubting immortality I still want to clinge to being remembered - at least for awhile by my family.

Jackie sometimes tells me I don't need her or anyone as much as she or others need people - I could get along even if some calamity took them all away. This was not said as a complaint, nor in anger, only as an observation of fact. Maybe so for this is the basis of the B.B. *(The Black Boar. This poem can be found on page*

123. The structure of the poem was influenced by James Dickey's poetry. I later met him when he did a reading at Vanderbilt.) Within my thoughts I am always muddling around with my own isolation & seperatness. Yet how I do enjoy being with & talking with friends. But do I really need them for themselves?

Yesterday our most prominent local financial wizard *(John Owens, an intense conservative)* was bemoaning the State of the Nations finances blaming inaptitude of past politicians & the unreasonable wage demands of labor. Hell. Like all striving to hold on when they're on top of the heap he just doesn't like loosing his money which comes to him constantly telling the public buy now - pay later don't wait till tomorrow. Manufacturers & Financiers & Advertising live off the need they must create. When the public is convinced of the need they then have to have money for purchase so they demand more money. Why can't those so omnipotent they must criticize others look critically at themselves & those like them? This was part of the greatness of M. Gandhi.

8/14/69 interesting conversation with Mr. Mayfield had come to our house reg. (Some carpentry work) who operates the Firetower Game Club *(See July 4, 1964 entry)* located one mi. from us on the firetower rd. For over ten years he has successfully operated a cock fighting eastab. There with only one raid, which he felt resulted from a dep. Sheriff who was men. disturbed (he later committed suicide). Mr M. was very open in describing history & handling of "chickens" but slightly evasive in explaining how he continued to be able to openly operate an illegal activity. Mr M is large, slow moving, doesn't look you straight in the eye but [for a] few seconds but appears rather kind & gentle. He says that he only pays a Fed. & State Amusement tax & the Club handles none of the gambling but only collects a gate fee. Also he keeps his crowds small & well mannered which limits behavior problems that could lead to trouble. He hinted at possible "payoffs" to some authorities. Says judge (Short?) knows of his operation & and if problems arise advises him what he should do. He rather proudly stated that his 2 sons had never been there (both grown - 1 teacher) due to his feeling they shouldn't be around gambling – no concern about the fights.

He originally obtained 100 chickens from a Virginia physician who "left" them with him & never wanted them back. He sells them all over the country & sometimes sends big ones 8 lbs. + to Japan. He described in some detail methods of breeding & conditioning & told me that inbreeding occasionally results in production of chickens similar to the Red Junglefowl (Asia) which is said to be the ancestor of all domestic chickens. Season reopens near Thanksgiving.

11/27/69 *Finally wrote a poem for Jackie*

It's Thanksgiving 1969 can be found on page 181.

2/1/70 at approx 10:00 PM coming home from church party we saw young male or small female bobcat walking in field (next to fence row) half way between Mr. Pearre's & Old Hillsboro Rd. Not startled by car lights but finally turned & disappeared into fence row bobbed tail easily seen by us all.

7/?/70 Sunday 11:30 AM 2 buck deer 11pts & 4 pts in velvet immediately beside Old Hillsboro Rd. headed toward Harpeth River approx. 1 mi past bridge & half mi before Forrest Home. All the children saw the.

10/11/70 Went to Jim Jones *(Jim and Nelda were friends from church)* & saw mounted golden eagle killed recently illegally at Monteagle, Tenn (near Lost Cove) probably with shotgun. Jim did not know details. His cousin an amateur taxidermist somehow acquired the eagle & was afraid of possible legal action & gave it to Jim. Mounted with wings spread, beak open & standing on limb - what a shame as it certainly must be one of the last eagles in that area - if not a transient. *(Jackie and her father and brother A.M. owned Lost Cove but later sold it. Now in 2012 the valley floor is owned by my friend Elizabeth Motlow Logsdon and the mountainside by the University of the South. Eagles are returning to Tennessee.)*

9/72 During summer saw 2 pure white does 1 with natural colored fawn 1 with 10 pt. Buck. *(The one with the fawn was in our neighbor's large field. Got two photographs of her. The other was miles away off Old 96.)* Deer population picking up - see them almost monthly. Acquired another bobcat skin from cat hit by car on Old Hillsboro Rd. Fewer snakes around house this summer tho last year we killed 3 rattlers (1 killed by Brad 2 by me) Area gradually changing as more people move out from Nashville. Survey for new Natchez Trace Parkway done this summer. Lynch is becoming quite a horseman & Trina, Adam & Darwin like to ride double. Adding on to house - recreation room & boy's room over garage.

6/11/78 *On this day, Sunday, Brad and Lynch in wreck, at the road entrance, in which two people died. We paid off a settlement in a civil suit and sold our house and land and we moved to Nashville.*

8/31/86 Now live in Nashville 1724 N. Observatory Dr.

Up 4:30 AM read. Church with Jackie & Darwin, then all to lunch with Fannie *(Elizabeth Crossley Spain, my mother),* Jane & Trish *(my sister and her daughter).* Cloudy, misty. Asthma, no energy, irritable. A.M.'s dtr. Christy moves in tonight - with us til parents move (our home seems to always have one or more extra - just to list a few black Wendell *(Lipscomb student)* slept in closet for months, cause his snoring woke Darwin, Annagrit from Germany YMCA last summer, Mike Brazil (Mary and George's son), one night a native Zambian woman who I never saw. Anyhow it prevents boredom. Discussed Adam and Angie's forthcoming marriage 12/20. *(Angie Dickenson, from near Liverpool. Adam met her while in the Marines and stationed in England.)* She's Catholic & he's Ch of Christ. How is the thing to be balanced - ah well Jackie can do it & do it well. Brad & Tina on 3rd western trip. *(Tina Poteet was Brad's wife. They later divorced.)* Lynch visited awhile (still has his DUI hanging over him) - he is loveable & would fight the world for us. Darwin (as usual) asleep upstairs. Trina is in & out awaiting call from her boyfriend - Catholic bluegrass guitarist - Pat. *(Pat Flynn. They married.)*

9/1/86 Labor day. Asthma & weakness continued. In bed much of day, a real grouch. Adam called [from England] to discuss more details for wedding. He'll be home from St. Mawgan Cornwall Eng. In 100 days. Cloudy, misty &

doldrums. Christy moved in last night - she's cute, so Darwin's pals will probably flock to us even more

9/2 Gray sky, rain & mist continue. At work but still ill, throat sore, no energy & less interest yet am suppose to carry out the roll of leader. *(Director of Columbia Area Mental Health Center)* When ill I get pessimistic about my work & undecided about our future - where should we live, what will give the most shared happiness to Jackie and me - obligations, obligations - I despair them yet realize they also represent fulfillment and money.

9/9/86 In bed sick 4 days, detached, no interest. Am losing a sense of caring about my work, friends, family. The exception is Jackie - I feel more dependent on her as my self assurance diminishes. My self centeredness is unhealthy & boring & yet outward goals & interests don't last. *(This is the final chronicle entry.)*

After the entry of 9/9/86 there is a long gap in the book then a number of literary quotations ranging from Samuel Johnson to William Faulkner. These were written between November 1969 and November 1970.

Finally, in Jackie's handwriting:

Snakes

1969
April, species uncertain, blueish gray
Color, about 2 feet long, caught near barn by Lynch

May 10, hog-nose, about 3 feet long,
Caught near Elam's old lake by George

May 11, black snake, 2 and half feet long,
Caught at Fannie's house by Mel

rat snake, 5 and half feet long (about)
caught by Elam's new lake spring house by Brad & Mel

black snake, about 3 feet long
caught at new lake by Brad,
found by Thunder (Beagle), Lassie (English shepherd) injured it, let go

earth snake, about 6", new lake,
Brad

Took all to Lipscomb Bio. Dept.

This is the end, but not for those we love--George

The Great Revival of 1953

Dedicated to the 1953
Graduate Saints and Sinners
Of David Lipscomb High School

I do not remember much, nor remember very well,
But this I know for truth and this I'll truly tell,
Every year in high school chapel,
There was held a Great Revival.
A preacher came and preached of sin
And fire, that sinners burned forever in.
It scared the you know what out of me,
As I think it did you, for I still see
Us all hunkered deep down in our seats
Trying to hide, while the preacher entreats
Us to, "Turn from Satan's way!
Come, come now; be saved this very day!"
Then with his piercing eye, he held me long,
And sang, and sang, and sang, the invitation song:

> *"Almost persuaded, harvest is past!*
> *Almost persuaded, doom comes at last!*
> *Almost cannot avail; almost is but to fail,*
> *Sad, sad, that bitter wail - almost but lost!"*

O Lord, I almost died of fright,
If *doom* did not strike me then, I knew it would that night.

I prayed, "Feet rise up and walk! Dear Lord, do not let them fail.
I promise, I swear, I hear that bitter, *bitter wail.*
Feet, damn you, move - and preacher keep on singing.
I'll come forward, if my feet will get to springing."
Then it happened, there went one of you, then two, then three and four,
Then more, and more, and more.
A host of teenage sinners went rushing down the aisle.
All their feet were working, and their faces all did smile.
My time was running out, with fervor I did pray,
But still my feet of stone did stay, and stay, and stay.

"Sad, sad that bitter wail - almost but lost."

"Lost...lost...lost," echoed clearly, finally...and was gone.
Then silence, but for a whimper, that from my mouth was drawn.
I prayed, "Great God Almighty, don't let that song end there.
I promise I'm *persuaded,* but my feet won't work, I swear!"
His answer to my prayer came quickly, "Perchance,
Doth thou not remember all thy sneaking 'round to dance?"
The moral of this story is: Feet can lead you straight to hell.
So, since then, to warn others, I tell my terrible tale.
For what I've told you is the truth you see.
It happened to me, and it happened to thee, thou Class of '53.

1993

...others were downright ridiculous...

An Aged and Aberrant Author's
Acrimonious Alliterations
Bad Eye
Cat's Cradle
Toes
The Rime of Ancient Boozer
Head Druid's Annual Entrails Readings

An Aged And Aberrant Author's Acrimonious Alliterations

Black Bob brazenly burped baloney breath, but Bucking Betty's big behind blew bouncing blue bubbles breaking Black Bob's belching bravado badly before Bobo Butterbutt bested both by belching bloody beef.

* * * * *

Mid medieval maiden-missing monasteries, mead-merry Monks mumbled Mass miserably; moreover, many maiden-martyred mind-maddened Monks made majestic Madonnas mercifully moan majestic Madrigals.

* * * * *

An angry aardvark attacked Alonzo A. Abussinian's abundant anatomy after abysmal Alonzo asserted, "Aardvark's ancestors ate artichokes" and, afterwards, abased Alonzo always avoided allegations about Aardvark appetites.

* * * * *

Certifiably convinced certain cosmic configurations confirmed Cheshire cats caused communism, Claude "Crazy Cat" Coley crucified cunning Cheshires, copying craftily Chauncey "Cheyenne" Curdog's carefree Christlike carvings.

Bad Eye

One night me and JoJo Pettibone were steady drinking Bud in this brick-o-block beer joint out on the county line when in walks a fellow JoJo had once worked with up in Detroit. JoJo yelled at him, "Hey, C.T., you no-count, egg-suckin' hound, get yore ass over here and lemme buy you a cold one, ole buddy." I'd never met C.T. but later on found out that his initials stood for "Chicken Thief", which was his nickname and which he had picked up while serving eleven-twenty-nine on the county road gang for stealing a semi loaded with three thousand White Leghorns.

From a distance, and because my vision was starting to blur, all I could see was this tall lanky guy with his head sunk down between a pair of hunched-up, bony shoulders, sort of like how a turkey buzzard looks. But it was when he sat down across from me, where I could really study him, that I began to get an uneasy feeling. He and JoJo were jawing away and laughing so hard about their auto working days that they were paying no mind to me. So I just kept sipping my Bud and studying C.T., trying to figure out exactly what it was about him that was bugging me. Then it hit me clear and hard, like an ax handle up side the head. My hands started shaking and I could feel the left side of my mouth twitching.

C.T. had one of them faces that had always unsettled me something terrible. Well, it wasn't exactly his face—it was his eyes. Every time I tried to look at them I could hear my mama saying, "Dooney Gene, if I've told you onct, I've told you a thousand times, when you're talking to someone don't look away, look them right straight in the eyes."

Well, that's what was unsettling. I couldn't tell which eye C.T. was behind because they both went off in different directions. While he was talking, C.T. seemed to be looking at me as much as he was looking at JoJo. I'd try to look at both of his eyes at the same time, but I couldn't get my own eyes to angle right, or spread out enough, or whatever it took. When I looked between JoJo's eyes I wondered if he thought I couldn't focus right. Then I tried honing in on one for a bit and then shifting over to the other and give them equal time. No matter which one I picked, it made me feel like I had the wrong eye, but there was one thing I was sure of—one of the eyes was a bad'un.

My mama's voice was really giving me a hard time. Sweat broke out on my forehead and I was beginning to get a tad angry. Something was starting to make me think there was a smart aleck behind the eyes making fun of me. It was like C.T. was jumping back and forth inside making the good eye look bad one minute and the bad eye look good the next.

It was just about then that a smart-ass grin lit up in his right eye. Man, I was fit to be tied! When it saw me staring all upset like, it suddenly ducked out and jumped over to the left one then it went to flipping that grin back and forth from eye to eye like a Mexican jumping bean. About the time I was certain which eye was grinning at me it jumped away and over to the other one.

It was right in the middle of one of those jumps that I busted C.T. smack dab between his good eye and his bad 'un—whichever one it was.

Cat's Cradle

Funny

how a straight piece of white string

with its ends

tied together

and woven

with the very best intentions

between eight fingers and two thumbs

on two hands

can end up

a bloody awful

mess

Toes

Almost every night your toes leave your feet,

They jump from the bed to the floor and meet

Other toes, to run, to jump and to play

All through the night 'til the next light of day,

When they hurry to climb back onto the bed,

And onto your feet and not on your head,

Big toe on one side, little on the other,

Three in the middle in the right order,

But when you awake, check each one with care,

So your father's aren't there, all covered with hair.

These lines were composed while I was drunk as a skunk, brought on by two six-packs of Budweiser taken to check a run of bad luck.

"S.T."* Coldwater

The Rime of the Ancient Boozer

I drink and drink and drink a lot,
But never use crack and never smoke pot.
The only joints I ever use
Are on the county line where I abuse.

Budweiser regularly and sometimes Schlitz,
They're also where I have my fits.
Strange things I've seen and stranger heard,
But the worst of all is the Great Speckled Bird.

It giggles and sings a song that's quite jolly,
And then, Hot Damn, it turns into Miss Dolly.
She plays her guitar and shakes her gold hair,
Then she turns into the bird and giggles, "Beware!"

I rub my eyes but still it's there,
Flapping and circling me in the air,
Singing beer ads like the ones on TV.
Then without fail it shoots a bird at me.

Once, I pulled my gun and shot it twice,
Then for good measure I shot it thrice,
And it just giggled and giggled, "Penance more you'll do,"
Then up around my neck it flew.

Now, I sit here a total wreck,
With this Great Speckled Bird around my neck,
It keeps goosing me with its tail,
And giggling, "It's fun to be with you in jail."

* "Severe Tremors" Coldwater

Head Druid's Annual Entrails Readings

On every twenty-first of June, all our folk
Gather together over at Big Oak,
For Head Druid's annual ox killing,
And Divine Order of Entrails Readings.

Entrails Readings used to be a super time,
Until Head Druid lost his mind;
There were ox ribs and mead, and sweet young girls,
And auguries augering better worlds.

But now, Head Druid is senile and has cataracts,
You can't trust his auguries always to be facts.
For example, I'll never believe him again when he sees,
Flights of eagles killed by bees.

Last year, he got us to believing we were those bees,
And get this, he convinced us those eagles were Roman armies.
Well that one got our arses whipped,
And I ended up hiding in a pit of shit.

Then there's those dumb-rocks he calls Stonehenge, that's where
He runs around in circles raving to the air,
"How does it go, how does it go...
Did I set it for Sun-ray...or was it Moon-glow?"

I don't let my children watch ox killings anymore,
There's too much violence, too much gore.
You're supposed to kill them with one whack,
But with Head Druid, it's HACK - HACK - HACK!

Since he got arthritis, he's lost his touch,
He drops the entrails entirely too much.
No wonder our future always looks scary,
The livers he reads are dirty and hairy.

Yesterday, when he announced he had crowned himself Head Fairy,
I decided that's enough, I'm moving over to Eire,
Where I hear St. Patrick is doing quite well,
And that it's a nice place to live, since he gave the snakes Hell!

...several were serious...

The Burial of Marcy McKenzie
Mustangs
My Extinction
Leningrad 1941 – 1942
Three Old Men on the Elk's Club Porch
Around the Courthouse

The Burial of Marcy MacKensie

The Winchester Chronicle - February 21, 1927

Following a brief illness, **Marcy Mary Mackensie** died yesterday at her home in Roark Cove where she and her large family have resided for many years. She will be buried at 1:00 pm tomorrow in the MacKensie-Jones Cemetery, located on her large farm, "Scot Land". "Miss Marcy", as those who knew her called her, was born in the Scottish Highlands on June 11, 1843. Her family immigrated to North Carolina in 1850. She is preceded in death by her first husband, Robert Campbell, and two children, Callie Elizabeth Campbell and Alexander Charles Campbell. She is survived by her second husband, John Thomas Jones, twelve children, seventeen grandchildren and eight great grandchildren. She was known for riding long miles on horseback to deliver babies in remote valleys and sections of the mountains, and for raising prize-winning Ayrshire cattle and Blackface sheep. Noted for her straightforward manner of speaking, she informed her children that when she died no preacher, or politician or citizen of England was to be allowed to attend her burial.

It was a miserable day; the kind of day Marcy MacKensie would have loved. Cold, misty days brought back the cold, misty happiness of her Highlands childhood.

The weather seeped into the bones of the two hundred or more mourners already gathered outside the cemetery's iron fence at the foot of the knoll where her open grave waited; they stomped their feet, turned up collars and pulled hats down against the gusts of wet and wind. More were coming along the footpath that led the two hundred yards from the castle across the open pasture to the knoll. Some of them Marcy had delivered as babies. They came for miles from the mountains and across the valley, some all the way from Winchester, a few from Nashville. They came in farm wagons, buggies and cars, some riding horses or mules, a few on foot.

The knoll was bare of trees. Surrounding its bottom was a ring of cedars and the iron fence. Five tombstones were at the top: three of Marcy's children and two of her grandchildren.

That morning there had been a spitting of snow and sleet. Now a steady mist had settled on the valley, shutting out the mountains. Marcy would have thanked God for it if she had thought He was there. She said bad weather gave her hope whereas bad people–which she believed most to be–were proof that God had created many mistakes. One was the English. She hated them. Because of an English landlord her family was driven from their land in the summer of 1850.

Her scorn for preachers and politicians came partly with her rise from poverty by back-breaking labor, saving her money and her exercising caution in spending it. As she told her children and grandchildren, "Thaur all leeches, livin off tha blood uv workin people. They dae no like tae sweat ur think, so they just suck tha blood out uv others. You could nae fill a shotgun shell with thair wee brains." And when she thought of the day her family was forced from their croft, she remembered with a curse that not one preacher or politician was there to help them. "I'll ne'er give em a penny, nae a vote, if they want anythin frae me they can come here an look at me bare arse."

She was born a big ugly baby with a full head of hair more orange than red. She grew to stand six feet tall and weighed a bit over two hundred and twenty-five muscled pounds. Long, tangled hair surrounding a fair-skinned, freckled face were all lumped together without beauty or softness with one exception: When she was delivering a baby, or nursing or playing with one of her own, her blue eyes became warm and soft, even beautiful.

"Havin bairns," she told her children, "whur tha reason I wus put on tha earth, tae bring them out uv thair mothers an tae hae me own...If nae fer needin a man tae hav them...an so me own nae be bastards, I'd nae taken any man as me husband, even yer own faithers."

She was seven when she and her parents and two older brothers sailed from Scotland. To assure they would never return, their landlord paid their six-week passage to North Carolina. There they were met by their father's distant cousin, John Cowan, who gave them a house and a small bit of land on the backside of his eight hundred acre plantation. From their open door they could see the dark wall of the western mountains.

Their one-room log house had one door, no windows. The floor was dirt and much of the chinking was gone. The roof's mossy shingles were rotten and the half-stone, half-stick chimney blew smoke back into the room at the slightest gust of wind. It stank of animals.

In their first year in America, her mother died in childbirth, leaving a baby daughter, Morna, to be raised by Marcy who was barely nine. Two years later, her father died of consumption. In the spring of 1862, her older brother was killed in Virginia, fighting with the 4th North Carolina Regiment at the Battle of Seven Pines. Her other brother was captured in the same battle and sent north to a Yankee prison. He never returned.

She was twenty-three when the war ended. Morna was fourteen. They were alone. They barely kept alive. With hoes they broke the ground, planted and grew just enough corn, potatoes and pumpkins and, with nets, trapped enough birds and animals for meat and from the fields and woods gathered enough plants, nuts and berries to stay alive.

Then their fate changed. For what was to happen, Marcy never thanked God. She had lost faith in Him after He had not answered her prayers and allowed so many of her family to die.

Like the MacKensies, Robert Campbell was a Highlander. He had come to America in 1825. He was a wealthy man, a very wealthy man with large herds of cattle and flocks of sheep, broad acres of corn and wheat, three mills, two ferries, a store and the largest house in western North Carolina. He owned no slaves.

In the heart of the winter of 1866, Robert's wife, Callie, died of fever. He was left with a three-year-old son, Ewan. He had no other family, no one to help raise his son. Two days after Callie's funeral, he rode twenty miles down the valley to see if his friend, John Cowan, knew of an available woman. Their talk was brief. It was Robert's nature to come straight to the point.

"John, dae ye know a lassie fur me tae take tae be me wife?"

"Ah, yes! I do! I do!"

"Will she be good tae me boy?"

"Ah, she will, she will."

"An whur will I find her?"

"Ye'll find her here, on me own land."

"An who be she?"

"Her faither wus uv me own blood."

"An what be her name?"

"Her name tis Marcy MacKensie."

And so it was, within that same month Morna MacKensie married John Cowan's oldest son, Donald, and Marcy married Robert Campbell, a man who, although forty years older than she, was to be the only man she ever loved. He was an old man and she an ugly woman, but they loved one another and were good lovers and had three children.

Oh, how she loved her babies! Every tenth or eleventh month a new one came. They were all girls. She named them after the women she loved: her mother, her sister and grandmother: Fiona, Morna and Kenna. She would have kept on having them but, the month after the third one was born, Robert was thrown from his horse and died two days later, never regaining consciousness. Though she had lost her faith, she prayed again, over and over, for Robert's life. Again, the answer was death. And with that, she decided she no longer believed God existed.

Now, she was a rich woman. She inherited everything. Soon, the suitors came in droves from miles away, from across the lowlands and the mountains, as though she was the most beautiful woman in North Carolina. Finally, she picked her next husband. He wasn't one of the suitors.

He was her employee.

John Thomas Jones had a weak chin; his shoulders slumped; he had thin hair, a scraggly beard and watery eyes that never looked directly at the person to whom he was speaking. 'John Thomas', as everyone called him, had achieved next to nothing in his twenty-four years. In fact, he was a poorly-paid clerk in what had been Robert Campbell's store and which was now Marcy's. He had never married and had few, if any, social graces. He was a weak man who survived in life by subservience to those whose wills were stronger than his.

He was just the kind of man Marcy wanted for a husband: a man who would give her more babies and not interfere with how she lived her life or her plans for the future.

Four months after Robert's death, Marcy galloped up to the front of Campbell's Store. Mounted as a man, she threw her right leg over the saddle and slid to the ground from the back of her seventeen-and-a-half-hand-high saddle horse. Her long orange hair hung in tangles around her shoulders. She tied the reins to the hitching post and gave her right leg a hard slap with her riding crop. Beneath her long black dress and jacket she wore dark-gray wool pants and high-top riding boots with small spurs that glinted for a moment in the sunlight. The wooden steps and porch creaked as she crossed them and strode rapidly inside without stopping and on toward the rear of the store and storage room, calling over her shoulder, “John Thomas, ye come on back here with me!”

“Yes’um," he said, moving quickly from behind the counter and following behind her, staring downward at the glitter of the spurs on the heels of her black boots. He was so scared his heart sat behind his teeth; she was either going to fire him, or beat him with the riding crop, or something worse.

Once inside the storage room she closed the door, turned to John Thomas, slapped the crop twice against her boot, took two steps toward him and said, “De ye know I be rich?”

Looking down at the toe of her left boot, he could barely get “Yes’um” out of his mouth.

“John Thomas, de ye luv bairns?”

“Yes’um, I guess. What do they taste like?”

“Nae, nae, nae. Children! De ye luv children?”

“Oh, yes’um, I love children, specially lil ones.”

“De ye have any?”

“No’m.”

“De ye hae a woman?”

“No’m.”

“De ye think ye’d be a good faither?”

“Yes’um, I suppose.”

"Well then, it be settled. Ye'll marry me next Saturday."

At 11:00 am, on Saturday, April 24, 1869, Marcy Mackensie and John Thomas Jones were married in the Buckhorn Presbyterian Church. As with Robert

Campbell, Marcy did not take Jones as her married name. Less than a dozen people came to the wedding.

Five months later, she sold the mills, ferries, store and everything in it, the livestock, farm equipment, the house, barns and land. The day after the final sale in early September, Marcy kissed Robert Campbell's headstone, waved over her shoulder as she walked away; then she, John Thomas, Fiona, Morna and Kenna started west into the mountains. They drove two heavily loaded wagons, each pulled by six oxen. Marcy's horse was tied to the rear of her wagon; two Jersey milk cows were hitched to the rear of John Thomas's. They headed for Tennessee and a thousand acres of prime land that Robert had bought as an investment.

The road was rough. It wound its way like a snake through the deep, narrow valleys, the dark walls of the mountains so near they could almost be touched. In the shade and beside the streams it was cool, but most days burned hot and were lonely and long. The oxen's massive shoulders steadily pulled the wagons, the wheels dropping in ruts then jerking out, scraping over rocks, jarring and shaking Marcy's big breasts and the baby within her.

Finally, they came out of the mountains into hills and open farmlands. They angled southward into middle Tennessee and on to the foothills of the Cumberland Plateau. There they came to her land: a broad level valley with good water, meadows, corn and wheat fields and some of the richest soil in Tennessee. She was six months pregnant. As she looked on the land her thoughts were long thoughts; she saw them and all that would be there, *"I'll nae be poor again. Ai! I'll work hard an have all tha wee ones I want...an I'll build me a castle."*

The castle was of limestone, sandstone and red brick, thick-walled, with two towers and a courtyard with gardens. There were leaded windows, iron hinges, stone floors and oak doors; it rose near the foot of the mountain at the south end of Roark Cove. In bright sunlight it shone red, orange and silvery brown; behind it the forest and mountains stretched away east, west and south, blue-black from a distance, deep green when near. In front and to the sides of the castle were cornfields, orchards and pastures with black-faced flocks and red and white mottled herds. And there were children and grandchildren and great grandchildren. And there was John Thomas, a good father and a poet with no poetic ability and, eventually, in his late fifties, a confirmed drunkard.

For fifty-seven years, Marcy MacKensie lived a happy life in Roark Cove. In her eighty-fourth year, she died in her sleep following a large meal of cottage pie, Haggis, two servings of Scotch trifle and two full glasses of red wine.

By 1:00 pm all the mourners had arrived. Standing in a semi-circle, they waited, cold and wet outside the iron fence. A few had umbrellas, some wore raincoats, many had on only their church clothes and hats. Scattered among them were men in overalls and work hats and women with worn coats, shawls and gingham dresses that hung down to the grass and mud. They looked back across the field toward the castle. A little ways off, the spotted cattle faced the mourners; now and then, a bell tinkled.

Through the gate, nearest the castle, came a farm wagon drawn by a matched pair of red mules. Three strides behind the wagon walked a piper playing *Flowers of the Forest;* behind him came the family, all with green, blue and black plaid armbands. Marcy's youngest grandson and youngest granddaughter drove the wagon. In the bed of the wagon, the mist made beads of silver on the dark walnut wood of the coffin. On the outer lid, directly above Marcy's face, her grandchildren had painted the MacKensie coat of arms: a blue shield with a stag's golden head and antlers.

Standing to the side of the mourners two bearded old men dressed in black whispered to one another out of the corners of their mouths.

"I law, she'uns whar a helluva woman!"

"Hell, she'd been a helluva man."

"Nairy a way you'd beat her on a trade."

"Lord God, you'uns better never try an cheat her. She'd fight ya."

"I hyar she never set foot in a church."

"I'd say that's likely."

"They'uns say she kilt a bar with an ax when hit took after her calves."

"That's likely too."

"I give her honor though, fer savin my Mary when she had our last un."

"She'uns could be an onry cuss but she'uns brung a lot of em that are standin hyar inta this world."

"Well, hyar she be."

The wagon stopped in front of the iron gate. The mourners moved to the side as eight grandchildren came to the rear of the wagon. The drivers let the back down and helped the others slide the coffin out. The ten of them carried it up the slope to the open grave. The piper and family filed behind. They filled the space within the cemetery. John Thomas's two oldest sons helped their father stay upright.

Every man removed his hat. Except for the cawing of a crow and the lowing of a cow on the far side of the pasture there was silence.

Then the piper began to play as the family began to sing Marcy's favorite song, just as she had taught them.

Bonnie Charlies's noo awa,
Safely ower tha friendly main;
Mony a heart will break in twa,
Should he ne'er come back again.

Will ye no come back again?
Will ye no come back again?
Better loved ye canna be,
Will ye no come back again?

Ye trusted in your Hielan men,
They trusted you dear Charlie.
They knew your hidin in tha glen,
Death or exile bravin.

Will ye no come back again?
Will ye no come back again?
Better loved ye canna be,
Will ye no come back again?

Sweet the skylark's note an long,
Liltin wildly up tha glen.
But aye tae me he sings a song,
Will ye no come back again?

Will ye no come back again?
Will ye no come back again?
Better loved ye canna be,
Will ye no come back again?

When the last words were sung, the last shovel of dirt was patted down on Marcy's grave and the last of the family and mourners had left the field, the cattle returned to stand where the mourners had stood and snowflakes began to mix with the mist.

Two years later, at age eighty-two, John Thomas self-published a slender volume of poetry. Of the three hundred copies only eleven were sold, and these to his children. This led to more drinking. Three months after his ninety-third birthday he was found dead, slumped over his writing desk. An empty bottle of Johnnie Walker stood beside an inkwell. Gripped in his left hand was a crumpled sheet of writing paper. On it, he had scrawled his final poem.

My extinction may come as a surprise,
Though it's happening before your eyes,
For strange as it may be,
I'm the very last one of me.

His family considered it to be the best thing he had written. It was read at his funeral. The weather was perfect. Fewer than a hundred attended. John Thomas Jones was buried on the left side of Marcy Mary MacKensie.

Mustangs

Sunset

Thank the good Lord you've finally come
Many made it but we lost some
We've come a long way
Let's stay here a while
We can sit and rest our legs
Climbing hills and mountains wears you out
Coming down those steep slopes ruined my knees
My back has given out
My feet are sore as hell
The worse things were those storms
Some were downright scary
They were awful just awful
Have you been through any
Ah yes I thought so I
I see it in your face
Turn around let me lift that heavy pack off your back
Now sit here by me on this soft moss
Let's lean our backs against this old oak
Ah boy that's better
Want a drink
Take a swig of this
It'll clear the dust out and perk you up
Let's rest awhile here with the others and listen to the quiet
Look at those rolling green hills
Frankly I can't walk another step til I rest
We still have a way to go
I'll bet a dollar there're more mountains ahead
And of course we've still got that last deep valley

WHAT DID YOU SAY
WILL YOU TALK LOUDER

Did you say I'm starting to talk gloomy
How in the world could I sound gloomy
I'm the one who wrote that famous funny ditty

My extinction may come as a surprise
Though it's happening before your eyes
For strange as it may be
I'm the very last one of me

You're not smiling
Do you feel left out
Well what if I include you

Our extinction may come as a surprise
Though it's happening before our eyes
For strange as it may be
We're the very last ones of we

How's that
You're still not smiling
I thought you used to have a sense of humor
Or...was that someone else

WHAT
WHAT DID YOU SAY

Oh you don't think much of my humor
Or of my memory
Or my hearing

Well you don’t have to get testy
You’re all worn out
You need to rest that solemn old face of yours

HOT DAMN

Please forgive my language
But did you feel that
The ground’s shaking

NO NO NO MY BOWELS AREN'T MOVING

THERE

There it is again
You felt it that time
Your eyes are popping out of your head
The Lord have mercy
It's shaking harder and harder

LISTEN...WHAT’S THAT
QUIT THAT WHIMPERING SO YOU CAN HEAR

Is it an earthquake or is that thunder
Whatever it is it’s coming our way and it’s coming fast
You’re damn right I’m getting up
Can you still climb a tree
O my gosh

WHAT IN HEAVEN'S NAME IS THAT

It sounds like whinnying and snorting

Forgive how I talk when I get excited but I can't help it

DAMNATION

That IS whinnying and snorting

THAT'S HORSES

O my gosh O my gosh Do you see what I see
O my gosh it's a herd of...

WILD MUSTANGS

They see us and are coming our way
O my gosh they're coming straight at us

WILD MUSTANGS

They are beautiful
They are magnificent
They are glorious

Glistening reds browns blacks dappled whites
Bucking rearing prancing
Whinnying whinnying whinnying
Twisting their strong necks
Shaking their great heads
Tossing their long manes
Raising their heads toward the sky
Their whinnying rises higher and higher
Into one long piercing note
Then ends

Slowly they walk toward us
They come closer and closer
Until quietly gently they are among us
They separate one by one until one of them stands beside each of us
Their big moist eyes look into ours
We see ourselves reflecting in their eyes
We run our hands over their warm powerful bodies
We grasp their manes
We pull ourselves upward onto their broad backs
We feel their strength in our hands and legs
We feel their muscles bunch and move
We press our heels to their sides and move forward
Walking trotting cantering galloping
Into the evening shadows

LOOK

Look there toward the skyline

See them

See those last golden rays fading into the darkening purple

My Extinction

My extinction may come as a surprise
Though it is happening before your eyes
For strange as it may be
I'm the very last one of me

Leningrad 1941 – 1942

Once
There were many children
Who were cold so cold
At night

Their thin arms clung tight
Around mothers
Who were cold   so cold

While terrible dreams
Were dreamed of food
That was cold   so cold
So very cold

Many little sleds
Squeaked over snow
That was quiet   so quiet

And no laughter
Was laughed by riders
Who were quiet   so quiet

While sliding   sliding
Toward a place
That was quiet   so quiet
So very quiet

O children
Of Leningrad
Beautiful Leningrad
Who are old   so old
So very old

May your children
Be warm with laughter

Three Old Men on the Elk's Club Porch

Three old men on the Elk's Club porch,
Rock on a summer's day.
The sun is hot but cannot scorch
Their daily rock away.

They rock forever and anon,
Through days of long ago,
An ancient rocking marathon,
Their tales rock to and fro.

Joe Bob decries the youth today,
"What are they coming to?
It's drugs and no respect I say,
We need to hang a few!

It's more hell and fire and brimstone,
The preachers need to preach,
And leave that socialism alone,
Which all the young ones teach.

Remember that old Campbellite?
He made you feel the heat.
Hell, I once wet my bed in fright,
And had to hide the sheet."

Just then, a funeral goes by.
Their rockers cease to rock
In honor of old friends who die.
Twelve - strikes the courthouse clock!

"Well, Squire, they're burying Miss Erma,"
Old Sam says kinda slow.
And Squire, who likes English humor,
Winks, "Yes, she's dead y'know."

Around the Courthouse

Old men
Sitting
Spitting
Old men
Sunning
Funning
Old men
Sassing
Gassing
Old men
Joking
Smoking
Old men
Piddling
Whittling
Old men
Lying
Dying

...and there is one who never leaves me.

Come Sit with me

My Last Breath

Come Sit With Me

What follows tells how the title of this book and this story originated. The events were written in my journal last year between May 22 and May 26. Now, almost a year later, I still have no satisfying explanation for what happened. My physician, who has known me for many years, believes what I experienced was a delayed reaction to loss. I am not convinced that is so.

George Spain, May 4, 2014

Wednesday, May 22, 2013. Something strange happened a few hours before sunrise this morning. I was in the den going through a stack of books piled on the footstool in front of me. The books contain letters and journals written by southern women before, during and after the Civil War. I was making notations from them for *Lucy Taggert's Six Letters,* a short story set between 1864 and 1878. I wanted to replicate, as nearly as possible, how women of that period wrote; not only what they wrote about but how they wrote it; what words they used that were unique to their time. Their letters were filled with matters of day-to-day living: God, illness, death, tidbits about their slaves whom they called "servants"; and always they were telling of their love for family and friends. Illness and death seem to be on every page–death from childbirth, battle, illness, accident and old age.

Open, on my lap was *The Children of Pride,* an exchange of hundreds of letters between members of a Georgia family during and after the war. Writing from

Savannah on June 25, 1865, Mrs. Mary Jones writes to her daughter, Mrs. Mallard in Atlanta:

> *The fearful condition of our armies on the front of our own state and Virginia fills every heart with trembling. Not a day now passes but we receive the sad tidings of some friend or acquaintance slain in battle. Our country is mourning many of her sons slain in battle. Rev. Mr. Andrews and his wife were in deep sorrow for the death of a promising son killed in Virginia. Your Aunt Julia trembles for her boys now on the battlefield. Colonel Joe McCallister is said to have died bravely...Major Thompson's remains are expected out in Liberty on Monday.*

As I read of these men's deaths I thought of our third son, Adam, who was killed in Afghanistan and–in that instant–I heard a sound, so faint and indistinct it was unidentifiable. I stopped writing and listened. It seemed to have come from the wall to my left. I turned and looked upward. In the dim light of the reading lamp I saw what appeared to be a small stain coming from beneath the ceiling molding. I thought, *Oh Lord, I hope that's not water,* then, out loud I said, "Well, hell, I've got to have some coffee; it can wait a minute." And I went to the kitchen.

Before continuing with what happened this morning; I need to tell about the den and what occurred here in May 2009. The room measures fifteen by fifteen feet with a nine-foot ceiling. There are two windows: one looks out on the front yard and my wife's flower garden; the other onto a smaller garden. There is a comfortable sofa under the window. The walls are painted dark salmon; bookshelves, packed with books, line three walls; much of the furniture is quite old; valuable books and family keepsakes are on the shelves of a large oak bookcase; paintings of Indians, tiger hunts in India, and one of Jackie's great grandfather hang on the walls; in a corner, behind a brass chandelier with four globes, are two carved wooden paddles–one painted–and bows and arrows and a blow gun from the Amazon. All in all, it is an interesting room filled with family history, as is most of the house. Our entire family loves to hear, and to tell, the stories of our family's past. Every stick of furniture, every painting and every artifact brought home from our travels have been divided up already among our children and grandchildren and will go to them when I die.

Jackie died of cancer in this room in the early morning of May 25, 2009. With help from Alive Hospice we cared for her as she lay in the bed that overlooked her garden; our children oversaw the morphine that kept her from hurting. She slept most of the time. Her skin color became a yellowish pallor; there was puffing and blowing from her lips; near the end there was a rattling in her throat; her eyes were semi-open but unseeing. I saw her last breath leave her mouth as she died. We had been married almost fifty-four years. We had five children, thirteen grandchildren and four beautiful great grandchildren.

Three hours after her death I sent this email to family and friends:

This morning at 5:22, Jackie died peacefully as she took a few soft shallow breaths. The children and I were at her side gently touching her and saying, "We love you." Flowers from her garden were in small vases on the window sill beside her and the first calling of the morning birds were just on the other side of the window. How wonderful it has been having her die in her own home with her family and Sally, her loving Lab, caring for her. The room has been filled with tears, quiet laughter and love. And, oh, how we loved her! It is something how we have loved one another all these years. My heart is broken but I tell you all, "My Lord, it's been a party!"

As I returned from the kitchen with my coffee the sound came again, this time slightly louder and longer and though still not clearly identifiable, it was rather like the deep inhaling and exhaling of someone breathing. As I stepped into the den it stopped. I set the cup down on the table beside my chair and turned on the bright chandelier lights. In the few minutes I had been out of the room the stain had grown. I got the stepstool, placed it next to the wall, stepped up and examined it. Its shape was rather like a flower petal; its deep purple color identical to the Siberian Iris—how ironic; this was Jackie's favorite color. I rubbed my fingers over the stain but felt no dampness. I sniffed my fingers; there was no scent. Whatever it was, was inside the wallboard.

I went back to the kitchen, got a ruler, came back and measured the stain: It was six inches from top to bottom, fives inches at its widest and a fourth of an inch at the bottom. I leaned forward until my nose was almost touching the wall and took in a deep breath but detected nothing.

"Well, it must be old age, like me...we're both falling apart: splotches on our flesh, bones creaking, bad plumbing and then along comes something weird."

I stepped down onto the floor, sat in my recliner, took a good sip of coffee and resumed reading letters and making notations.

Thursday, May 23, 2013 This morning, at exactly 3:30, as I was making up the bed, I heard the breathing–if that is what it was–it was louder and longer. I hurried to the den; just as I switched on the light the breathing stopped. I looked at the wall. The stain was larger. I climbed the stepstool and examined it through a magnifying glass and measured it. It had doubled in size. Magnification revealed only the deep purple; there was still no texture or odor. It measured twelve inches long by ten inches wide at its widest point and tapering to one half inch at the bottom.

Since Jackie and Adam's deaths, my daily life has become rather predictable and, except for my writing, uneventful. There is a certain comfort in this, but now it is being disturbed. I don't know why I don't simply call someone to investigate the stain. There must be a perverse curiosity in me to see if I can discover for myself what's causing these things. But then this question enters my mind: Can it be that something is happening in my brain: a slight stroke, early dementia? Or is it psychological? Has my routine, day-to-day life become so humdrum that I'm getting a peculiar enjoyment from the, as yet, unexplainable sound and stain? I remember Jackie once asking me, "Can't you ever give your mind a rest?" I don't think I gave her the right answer when I replied, "No, I can't." These strange happenings have entered my mind much like the first hint of a new story that has no direction or conclusion, only the curiosity to see where it leads. So, for the present, I'll continue my observations and measurements. As with most things that are out of the ordinary there will likely be a simple explanation. Now to bed.

Friday, May 24, 2013 It woke me again. The breathing. This time there was something more. After several breaths there was what sounded like the whisper of a word, maybe two; if they were words. I could not understand them. As before, it stopped as I entered the den. I switched on the light. The stain has doubled in size again. It is now halfway down the wall; it extends behind two pictures. Yesterday, I bought the strongest magnifying glass I could afford. I picked it up from the table. As I started to the wall, three things caught my attention: the large French print of flowers and an oil painting of cattle in a field were slanted downward toward the sofa and there was something that brought a sharp coldness–the sofa's cushion, nearest the stain, had an impression as if someone had been sitting there; I placed a hand on the cushion; it was still warm. How could that be? No one else was in the house. I took my hand away then put it back, there was no warmth. I smoothed out the wrinkles, then stepped up on the stool and examined the stain with the magnifying glass.

My God, I could see inside the stain—it glowed and was moving. I jerked backward and almost fell; I stepped down quickly, went to the bathroom and splashed water on my face. In the mirror I could see my fear. I dried off, went back to the den and looked through the glass at the stain again; the glow and movement were gone.

Am I hallucinating? Am I going mad? Tomorrow, May the twenty-fifth, will be the fifth anniversary of Jackie's death. Is she...

Sunday, May 26, 2013 I have no explanation for why I wrote nothing yesterday. The following is all I recall -

At 5:15, I was awakened by the breathing and with it a faint voice talking. I held my breath, listening, straining to hear what was being said; the words came between the breathing, but they were spoken so softly I could not understand them. I got up and hurried into the hallway. I could see light coming from under the closed door to the den. When I had gone to bed the door had been open and the reading light turned off. I reached out to the doorknob; as I was about to grip it, I stopped and pulled my hand back.

I had dreamed of Jackie and Adam the night before. They were walking side by side down the old wagon road that winds through Lost Cove. I was following a good way behind. They stopped, turned around and motioned for me to come on. I began to run toward them and then I woke up. Though I do not believe in spirits or ghosts, I do believe that dreams may at times speak to us of our longings. I do not dream of them often but there are times, in the early morning, when I am reading in the den, that I suddenly want to see them, so I conjure them up in my mind. She is as she was those last months; I hear the shuffle of her slippers coming down the hall to the door and, as the door opens, I see her standing there smiling at me and in her soft southern voice she says, *I'm coming to sit with you, Bubbas...my Precious.* Then Adam will be standing there beside her; big and bearded, he is wiping the sleep from his eyes. And sometimes I get up and go to them with my arms out and hug them to me.

I reached out and this time gripped the knob and turned it. As the door opened, I was blinded by light; from the room came a softness of air upon my face and the fragrance of flowers and honey; within the light I heard her, *My Precious, Come sit with me.* I stepped into the room and closed the door.

My Last Breath

You help me to my death
even as my last breath
now leaves me
you are here lifting me
through the air

www.ingramcontent.com/pod-product-compliance
Lightning Source LLC
Chambersburg PA
CBHW020553310726
48979CB00008B/1203/J

* 9 7 8 1 6 2 8 8 0 0 3 7 1 *